sketches

sketches

ERIC WALTERS

VIKING

VIKING
Published by Penguin Group
Penguin Young Readers Group, 345 Hudson Street, New York, New York 10014, U.S.A.
Penguin Group (Canada), 90 Eglinton Avenue East, Suite 700, Toronto, Ontario, Canada
M4P 2Y3 (a division of Pearson Penguin Canada Inc.)
Penguin Books Ltd, 80 Strand, London WC2R 0RL, England
Penguin Ireland, 25 St Stephen's Green, Dublin 2, Ireland (a division of Penguin Books Ltd)
Penguin Group (Australia), 250 Camberwell Road, Camberwell, Victoria 3124, Australia
(a division of Pearson Australia Group Pty Ltd)
Penguin Books India Pvt Ltd, 11 Community Centre, Panchsheel Park,
New Delhi – 110 017, India
Penguin Group (NZ), 67 Apollo Drive, Rosedale, North Shore 0632, New Zealand
(a division of Pearson New Zealand Ltd.)
Penguin Books (South Africa) (Pty) Ltd, 24 Sturdee Avenue, Rosebank, Johannesburg
2196, South Africa

Penguin Books Ltd, Registered Offices: 80 Strand, London WC2R 0RL, England

First published in Canada by Puffin Canada, a member of Penguin Group (Canada), 2007
First published in the United States of America by Viking,
a division of Penguin Young Readers Group, 2008

1 3 5 7 9 10 8 6 4 2

LIBRARY OF CONGRESS CATALOGING-IN-PUBLICATION DATA
Walters, Eric, date–
Sketches / by Eric Walters.
p. cm.
Summary: After running away from home, fifteen-year-old Dana finds friends on the Toronto
streets, and, eventually, a way to come to terms with what has happened to her.
ISBN 978-0-670-06294-2 (hardcover)
[1. Runaways—Fiction. 2. Homeless persons—Fiction. 3. Sexual abuse victims—Fiction.
4. Emotional problems—Fiction. 5. Toronto (Ont.)—Fiction. 6. Canada—Fiction.] I. Title.
PZ7.W17129Sk 2008
[Fic]—dc22
2007023123

Publisher's note: This book is a work of fiction. Names, characters, places, and incidents either
are the product of the author's imagination or are used fictitiously, and any resemblance to
actual persons living or dead, events, or locales is entirely coincidental.

Printed in U.S.A.
Set in Janson Text

AUTHOR'S NOTE

I GREW UP in Toronto in a single-parent family in an area just by the stockyards. It was a rough and tumble sort of neighbourhood populated by so many people experiencing life issues that were overwhelming—so overwhelming that many people just didn't make it. Instead they were crushed. They fell by the wayside, disappeared into the cracks, went to jail, became addicted to drugs and alcohol, died, or simply gave up or faded away to live a life so much less than what could have been—*should* have been. Many of them were good, decent people. All they needed was a hand to pull them up, somebody to believe in them, to offer a few words of encouragement, or a few dollars that would have made all the difference. Nobody was there.

Sketches is a work of fiction based on a real place—Sketch. I made up the people in this book, but I didn't make up the situations. Those are real. Thank goodness there are places like Sketch where they realize that homeless people are *people*, street kids are *kids*, disadvantaged youths are *youths*. I don't see Sketch so much as a building as an outreached hand. My special thanks to Rudy Ruttimann, Phyllis Novak, and the rest of the staff of Sketch for doing what they do to make the world a better place and for offering me their hands to help make this book work.

sketches

chapter one

"EXCUSE ME," I said as the woman walked up. She was middle-aged and well dressed in a sort of business outfit. I took a deep breath. "I have to get home and, I feel so stupid, but somehow I lost my money for the subway . . . it must have fallen out of my pocket . . . and I was wondering if maybe you could spare some change . . . I don't need much."

She stopped walking and stood in front of me, listening. Stopping was a good sign. Listening was a better sign.

"I already have a dollar so I only need another eighty-five cents."

She looked hesitant, like she wasn't sure she should believe me but didn't want to risk *not* believing me.

"And I know my mother is going to be so worried if I'm not home soon," I added, trying to sound desperate and genuine at the same time.

The woman looked like she was old enough to maybe have a daughter my age.

"And if I got *another quarter*, I could even call home to let my mother know what happened and why I'm late, because I'm *never* late . . . I've *never* done anything this stupid before, and I feel so bad begging for money and she worries so much and—"

"That's all right. I understand. Here you go," the woman said as she reached into one of the pockets of her jacket and pulled out a dollar and a quarter.

"Thank you so much!" I beamed. "You're such a nice lady. I'll just call my mother right now and let her know!"

The woman flashed a big smile back and then walked away into the subway station and disappeared down the stairs. I stuffed the change in my pocket.

"You really are quite the little actor."

I turned around. It was my friend Brent. "Thank you," I said, and gave a little bow from the waist.

"How much have you got so far, Dana?" Brent asked.

"That makes eleven dollars," I said, thinking about the money I'd already collected and stuffed in my pocket.

"That's not bad," he said. "Ashley said she's got about five bucks."

Ashley was another of my friends—actually, she and Brent and I were more than just friends, we were sort of a street family. Ashley wasn't far away. She was working one of the other two entrances to the subway.

"How about you?" I asked.

"Less than two bucks."

"Is that all?" I asked.

He shrugged. "Chicks always get more money."

"Yeah, right, it's really a girls' world, isn't it?" I said sarcastically.

"People just feel sorry for a girl out here begging for money. With me, they're sometimes afraid."

I could understand that. Brent was a big guy, tall, with broad shoulders. He looked like a football player, and when he put on his "mean" face he looked like somebody you wouldn't want to mess with. I knew that he was really a gentle guy who wouldn't hurt anybody . . . at least, not anybody who didn't try to hurt him or me or Ashley first. I'd already seen him jump in once when a guy started hassling Ashley. Brent threatened to tear his head off, and the guy took off pretty quick.

"Couldn't you just scare them into giving you money?" I asked.

"Doesn't work. Pity works better than fear, and you look pretty pathetic."

"Thanks . . . I guess. But if it's just a girl thing, then how come Ashley hasn't got more money?" I asked.

"She's not as believable as you."

"What does that mean?"

"You really look like you *did* lose your money, you know, like if somebody gave you a buck you really would get on the subway and go back to your house in the suburbs," he explained.

"That's *not* going to happen," I snapped.

"Yeah, but you just *look* like that. I guess that's because you haven't been on the streets very long." Brent sounded tired when he said that.

It certainly seemed like a long time to me. It was just over three weeks since I'd run away from home, but it felt like three months, or three years, or even three lifetimes ago. In some ways it wasn't even like I'd run away at all. I'd just got on a bus, thinking I needed to kill some time—I didn't want to get home before my mother did, not if my stepfather was going to be there. And that bus led me to another, which led to another, and then to the subway, and four hours later, there I was—in the city, and thirty miles from home. At that point it was way past my curfew and I didn't think I could retrace the steps to get home even if I'd wanted to.

Of course all I had to do was make a phone call and my mother would have come down and got me. Or told my stepfather to come and pick me up. But I wasn't calling anybody. Every time I passed a phone booth I knew I *could* call, but I didn't.

The first night on my own was scary. I stayed awake for most of it, drifted off for a while in a booth at an all-night doughnut shop, and finally fell asleep in a corner of the bus station, hidden behind some lockers. Nobody noticed me there. It was like I was invisible. Unfortunately, my backpack wasn't invisible. When I woke up it was gone, along with all my schoolbooks, a drama assignment due the next day, and my favourite sweater. Well, I sure as hell wasn't sweating the school stuff at that point, but the sweater would have come in handy. Thank God I'd kept my wallet in my pocket. I used my bank card to take out some money—forty bucks—and got some breakfast. If I'd known that they were going to cut off my bank card I would have taken out as much money as possible. I just didn't see it coming. That was so much like *him*—controlling, interfering, taking what wasn't his. He probably figured they could force me back home if they cut off the money—*my* money—the money I'd earned babysitting. There was almost six hundred bucks in there and I couldn't get it. What right did they have to do that?

What they didn't know was that when I found out the next day that the card had been suspended, I'd actually been trying to take out money to get a taxi home. I was scared and I just wanted to go home. But cutting off my card made me get angry, and that anger kept me away.

That was the day I ran into Brent and Ashley. Ashley was begging for money, using the same story we were using today. Maybe Brent didn't think she was believable, but she sounded pretty convincing to me. Even *I* gave her a dollar—hey, she was that good! Or maybe I was just afraid not to—she was also pretty scary looking.

Half an hour later she came up to talk to me. She'd noticed that I was just hanging around. She talked to me and then introduced me to Brent. At first I was pretty nervous, wondering if I could trust them. But really, what choice did I have? It was more scary to be alone than to trust those two, so I swallowed my fear.

Now, three weeks later, I don't know what I would have done if they hadn't taken me under their wings. Maybe I would have had to go home . . . No . . . I was *never* going home.

Brent interrupted my thoughts. "No offence, but you still look like a nice little girl from the suburbs."

"I look like a nice little girl from the suburbs who hasn't washed her hair in two weeks," I pointed out.

"It doesn't look that bad," he said.

"Thanks for the compliment, just the words I've always wanted to hear—'Your hair doesn't look *that* bad.'"

"You know what I mean. Ashley just looks more *street* than you do."

No argument there. I understood what he meant. Ashley was pretty, but there was a hardness to her. Her hair was still a little bit of half a dozen different colours it had been over the past months, and I wasn't really sure which—if any—was the real colour. She looked kind of tough, and tired. Life on the streets meant never getting enough sleep.

Ashley had told me she'd been out on the streets for almost six months . . . *this* time. She'd run away a dozen times, the first time when she was only twelve. Now that she was sixteen, I guess, technically, she wasn't on the run because she was old enough to live wherever she wanted.

"You live on the streets long enough and it changes the way you look . . . and the way you look at things." Brent sighed. Then he took a deep breath and stood up a bit straighter, as if he was giving himself a mental kick in the butt. "Anyway, back to work."

"Good idea," I agreed. "You'd better try a little harder and get a few more bucks. So far, I know that *two* of us have enough money to eat tonight . . ."

"Thanks for the encouragement," he said.

"I'm just joking . . . you know that, right?" I asked.

He smiled, turned, and disappeared around the corner of the subway station, heading back to the entrance he was covering.

I had to get back to work myself. I saw another woman walking toward me. I took a deep breath. This wasn't easy. It still gave me a bad feeling in the pit of my stomach—but not as bad as the hunger pain I was stuck with if I didn't do it.

"Excuse me," I said, "I was just wondering if—"

The woman brushed right by me, not making eye contact, not slowing down, acting like she hadn't seen or heard me.

"Jerk," I mumbled under my breath. She turned around and scowled at me. *That* she'd heard. Thank goodness she kept walking.

Two women clutching bundles of shopping bags approached.

"Excuse me, I hate to bother you, but I lost my money and I have to get back home, and I was wondering if either of you had any spare change so I could take the subway. I'm already late and my mother is going to be *so* worried."

"She *should* be worried, letting a girl your age come downtown by yourself," one of the women said. "How old are you? Fourteen?"

"I'm sixteen," I lied.

"This is a dangerous town for a sixteen-year-old," she continued. "You can meet all sorts of people on these streets . . . people a young girl like you really shouldn't meet."

"I *am* a little scared," I said, trying to sound convincing. That wasn't much of an act. There had been very few times since I'd left home that I *wasn't* at least a little scared. "I just want to get home before it gets dark," I said, adding a desperate note.

"Oh, that would be *awful*! I don't even want to imagine my little girl out here by herself . . . I don't think she'd even know what to do. Let me look for change," the woman said. She put down her shopping bags and then began rummaging through her purse.

"I have lots of plastic and bills, but nothing smaller than a twenty. How about you, Doris?" she asked the second woman.

"I can check." She put her bags down too and began looking through her purse. "Here we go!" she said, and she pulled out a ticket—a subway ticket!

"Gee, thanks!" I was trying to hide my disappointment. I'd thought I might get that twenty-dollar bill, and now I had a subway ticket. What good was a subway ticket?

She pressed it into my hand and then picked up her shopping bags.

"Now you hurry home before you give your poor mother a nervous breakdown. You kids have no idea how hard it is to be a mother!"

"That's right, Doris, no idea. I keep saying to my Angela that she won't know the grief she's caused me until she has children of her own!"

"Thanks for the ticket," I said, and started to walk away.

"Wait!" one of them called out.

I stopped and turned around.

"Aren't you going the wrong way? The subway is this way."

"Um . . . yeah . . . I know," I said. "I just want to call my mother before I leave. I know she'll be worried and I want to phone her." I pointed to a phone booth at the corner and I started to walk away again.

"Ahhhh," I could hear the woman say. "Such a considerate girl."

"Yes, considerate . . . but maybe she could wash that hair a little more often," added Doris as they walked away.

If what she'd said hadn't been so funny, and so true, I might have felt insulted.

I did feel really grungy. I also felt hungry. We hadn't had anything except a coffee and a doughnut each today. And I was also sore from sleeping on the ground or on concrete floors. At least I wasn't cold right now, but that would change when the sun went down. June had warm days, but the nights were still pretty cool, even downright cold.

Once I was sure the two women had made their way down the stairs to the subway I returned to my spot right in front of the doors. Another man came up toward the subway.

"Excuse me, I was wondering—"

"If I could spare some change so you can get home because you lost your money," the man said, cutting me off.

"Um . . . yeah . . . that's right," I stammered.

"Yeah, right, but it's not the truth," he said. "And the reason I know is that maybe you don't remember *me* but I remember *you*, and that's the line you used when you stopped me and I gave you money a couple of days ago."

"You gave me money?" I asked. This was the only time we'd worked at this subway station.

"At the next station on this line. I gave you a dollar!" he snapped.

He did look familiar.

"I already gave you a dollar," he repeated.

"Well, that explains it," I said. "If you'd given me a dollar eighty-five I could have gotten home." I walked away before he could react.

Brent had said that as long as we didn't work the same station too often we wouldn't run into the same people. That certainly sounded like a good theory. Too bad it didn't work. I spun back around, saw that the man had gone into the subway, and headed back to my spot once again. I didn't want to—not after that little exchange—but what choice did I have if I wanted to eat?

It was starting to get busier. People streamed by. Mothers with small children, business people rushing home, and university students carrying backpacks. There wasn't much point in asking the university students for money because some of them had less cash than I did. After begging for change the past few weeks I'd pretty much figured out who was a waste of my time. You looked at their eyes—did they make eye contact, or try to look away, or just pretend I wasn't even there? Or you could tell by how fast they were walking. The faster they were moving, the less chance that they'd drop some money in my hand.

A man in a business suit, carrying a briefcase, walked toward me. He was moving slowly and looking right at me. He had a sort of smile on his face. All good signs.

"Excuse me, I lost my money and I was wondering if you had some spare change so I could buy a subway ticket and go home. My parents will be really worried if I'm not home soon and—"

"How much do you need?" He stopped and put his brief-case down on the sidewalk. He reached into his suit pocket and pulled out his wallet. As he opened it up I could see that there was a wad of bills!

"Um . . . I don't need much . . . just a dollar or two . . . that would pay for my subway ticket, and I could make a phone call home as well to let them know I'm okay."

He pulled out two twenty-dollar bills. "I don't have anything smaller. Are you sure all you need is a couple of dollars?" he asked.

"Well, I . . ."

"Maybe you could take a taxi home instead of the subway, and get there faster."

"That would be *really* nice, *really* nice," I said, barely able to believe that he was offering me all that money.

"How old are you?" he asked.

"I'm almost seventeen."

"Oh . . . I thought you were younger, but that's okay."

He offered the money to me, and I reached out to take it, but he suddenly pulled his hand away.

"Do you want the money? All forty dollars?" he asked.

I nodded my head.

"Okay, but you have to answer a question for me," he said.

"What do you want to know?" I asked hesitantly.

"And if you're honest you can have the money."

"Yeah, what do you want to know?"

"You're not really going home, are you?"

I didn't know what to say. What did he want me to say?

"You're living on the streets, right?" he asked.

What was the point in denying it? He knew. I nodded my head.

"That's what I thought," he said. "And you're really not seventeen."

Again I nodded.

"How old are you?"

"Fifteen." I paused. "Almost fifteen," I admitted.

"That's a *nice* age . . . maybe a little older than I like, but still nice. Come with me."

"Come where?" I asked, feeling scared and a bit creeped out now.

"Let's just go over to that alley right over there." He pointed off to the side. "It'll just take a few minutes . . . you and me . . . and you get your money."

My eyes widened in shock and surprise. Finally I understood what he meant. I stepped back.

"Don't you want the money, little girl?"

I shook my head and staggered back a few more steps.

"What's wrong, you want more than forty dollars?" he asked. "Come on, sweetie, we're only talking four or five minutes . . . you're cute . . . and I like 'em young . . . but nobody's worth more than forty bucks for a few minutes."

A shudder went through my entire body.

"Well, what do you say, honey?"

I took a deep breath. "What I say . . . what I say . . . is that you're a *freaking creep*!"

"Keep your voice down," he hissed.

"I'm not doing anything you say, you *pervert*!" I screamed.

"Please, be quiet . . . you can have the money," he said, reaching out to me with the twenties.

"I don't want your money!" I shrieked as I slapped his hand. The two bills fluttered to the ground.

"You should be arrested!" I screamed. People all around us were turning and staring and gawking. I didn't care!

"What's going on here?" a loud voice demanded. I turned around. It was a policeman! "What's going on?"

Boy, was this guy going to be in trouble. Maybe the cop would arrest him, or—

"Thank goodness you're here, officer!" the man exclaimed.

I stared in shock. Why would he be glad that the cop was here?

"Did you hear what she was yelling at me?" the man demanded.

"Everybody on the street heard it," the cop said. He turned to the crowd that was gathering around us. "There's nothing to see here . . . all of you get moving." Hesitantly, reluctantly, the people started away and the crowd dissipated.

"What, exactly, is happening?" the cop asked.

"She was threatening me!" the man said. "This little street tramp was begging for money, and when I wouldn't give her any she threatened me! She said she'd claim I made sexual advances toward her. I offered her forty dollars to just be quiet, and she demanded more! She said she'd make me regret not co-operating, and you heard her with your own ears."

My mouth dropped open. I was too shocked to even think of what I could say.

"And I'm the *last* person in the world to do what she's accusing me of," the man continued. "I'm a businessman . . . I have a daughter of my own her age . . . I'm a property owner—"

"You're a liar and a pervert!" I yelled, my brain and mouth finally snapping back into gear.

"I am nothing of the sort, you filthy little piece of street trash! You should be arrested!"

"*You* should be arrested!"

"The only thing I am guilty of is being idiotic enough to stand up to your blackmail. I should have just given you more money like you demanded and gone on my—"

"Enough!" the policeman yelled, cutting him off mid-sentence. He looked at the man and then he looked at me. His gaze was hard and angry, and I lowered my eyes to the ground. The two twenties still lay there on the pavement.

"Were you begging?" the cop demanded.

I didn't know what to say.

"Answer the question!" he snapped angrily.

I nodded.

"It's illegal to beg for money. I should run you in. In fact, I should probably bring you in anyway, just in case someone actually gives a damn about you and filed a runaway report."

If he arrested me they'd call my mother, and then I'd have to go home. My right hand slipped up the sleeve of my left arm. My fingers rubbed against the slight ridges that crisscrossed my arm. Somehow it felt almost reassuring—

"Shouldn't she be arrested for trying to extort money, too?" the man asked.

"Sir, I think that—" the officer began.

"I'm just so glad you believe my story," the man said, interrupting.

"I didn't say that," the officer replied sharply.

I did a double take. He was staring at the man with that same hard, cold glare he'd aimed at me. He didn't believe what he was saying—he knew it wasn't true.

"Are you calling me a liar?" the man demanded of the officer.

"I'm not calling you anything."

"I'm a taxpayer! *I pay your salary* and I demand to know your name and badge number!"

"You want my badge and name, do you?" the officer asked.

"Immediately!"

The cop chuckled. "You'll get both of those," the officer said. "They'll be on your arrest report for solicitation."

The man's eyes got as big as saucers.

"Solicitation *of a minor*," the policeman added.

"But I wasn't doing—"

"Yes you were!" the officer snapped, cutting him off. "And if you argue with me any more I might just find something else to charge you with."

The man looked as though he was about to say something else, but he shut his mouth instead. He looked so terrified that I almost felt sorry for him—almost.

"I've been on the streets a long time," the officer said. "And I *ain't* no idiot." He paused. "Now, we have two choices." He paused again. "I can write this up . . . or we can all just walk away."

"I can leave?" The guy must have been scared, because now he sounded like he couldn't believe his ears.

The officer nodded. "I'll even walk you to the subway to make sure you get on your way *safely*."

Walk *him* to the subway? Was this guy joking?

"Thank you so much, officer, thank you. I'll do that right now, I'll leave, I'll go, I promise!"

"And since you're going, we won't need to continue our conversation about what you could be charged with, and how that might play out in court, and with your family, and in the newspapers, and on the evening news, and with your employer. Understand?"

"I understand . . . thank you, thank you," the man sputtered.

The officer turned to face me.

"And you, beat it, or I'll arrest you for begging and prostitution."

"Prostitution? I would never—"

"Don't you go lying to me too. You live on the street, you end up hooking, sooner or later. Now, I'm walking this guy to the subway platform to make sure he gets on his way. If you're still here when I get back, you can *count* on being arrested. You understand?"

I nodded my head dumbly. Everything just kept turning around so fast it felt like my head was spinning!

"And I don't want to see you around here *ever* again," he said. "Matter of fact, if I see you hanging around the streets—my *streets*—being arrested will be the least of your worries . . . if you know what I'm saying. So beat it!"

The cop spun back around and he and the man started for the subway entrance. I staggered away a few feet and then stopped. The two twenty-dollar bills were still there in the dirt beside the sidewalk.

"Dana, are you all right?" Brent and Ashley were right there. I guessed they'd been waiting for the officer to clear out.

"We've got to get out of here, before the cop comes back," I stammered. I burst into tears.

Brent threw his arms around me and I felt protected and safe.

"That . . . that . . . freaking pervert . . . did you see him?"

"Was he the guy with the cop?"

I nodded. "He wanted to give me money . . . money for . . . forty dollars . . . it's there," I said, turning around and pointing to the ground.

Ashley rushed over and grabbed the two bills from the ground. "Here," she said, offering them to me.

"I don't want his money!" I yelled.

"Take it easy," Brent said. "We *do* want his money." Ashley handed him the bills.

"We have to leave," I said. "We have to get out of here before the cop gets back or he'll arrest me." I struggled free and Brent released his grip.

"Come on, let's get out of here," Ashley said. She walked away, and I started to follow, until I realized she was leading us toward the alley the man had pointed at.

"I don't want to go that way," I said as I stopped in my tracks.

"We can go any way you want. Let's just not stay around here," Brent said. "Come on." He grabbed me by the arm and led me off in another direction, away from both the subway and the alley.

"Looking on the bright side, at least we have enough money now to get a really good meal and a couple of packs of smokes, maybe some entertainment," Brent said.

"What do you mean by 'entertainment'?" I asked.

"Maybe something to get high . . . a nickel bag, maybe," Brent explained. "We have the money for it," he said, holding the two twenties aloft.

"That's *my* money!" I said, and I grabbed it from him.

"I thought you didn't want it . . . ?" Ashley questioned.

"I don't . . . I mean, I didn't . . . but now that we have it, I know what we should do with it," I answered.

"What do you want to do?" Brent asked.

"I don't want to sleep in some abandoned building tonight. I don't want to sleep in a squat. I want us to get a room for the night. Someplace with a bed and a bathroom and a shower. Someplace where I can wash my hair."

"A shower would be nice," Ashley agreed. She turned to Brent. "Do you know any place we can get a room for the night for forty bucks?"

"I know a place where we can get a room for twenty-five."

"Twenty-five? Are you sure?" I asked.

"It's not exactly the Holiday Inn," he said. "It's on the Lakeshore strip. I know the guy who works nights on the desk."

"Is it a nice room?" I asked.

"It's a twenty-five-dollar room," he said. "But it's a lot nicer than any of the places we've stayed in for the last few weeks. And we'll still have money left over for at least ciga-rettes, and maybe something else."

"As long as we have some money left over after we eat," I said.

"I'd rather have smokes than food," Brent commented.

"Smoking is disgusting," I said.

"Yes, Mother."

"I don't know why anybody would smoke."

"I'm trying to impress my peer group," Brent joked, and despite my tears I started to laugh.

"Just my luck, I get to hang out with the only runaway in the world who doesn't smoke," Brent said, shaking his head.

"How about you just shut up and lead us to the motel."

chapter two

BRENT OPENED THE MOTEL ROOM DOOR with a flourish. He stepped inside and flicked on an overhead light. The room was tiny, and even with the light from the single bulb it looked dingy and dark. We followed him in.

"It smells," Ashley said.

It did have a strange odour—sort of like musty, damp mothballs.

"I'll open a window." I threw back the curtains to reveal a dumpster sitting in the parking spot directly across from us. Nice view. And it turned out the windows were nailed shut. Then again, what was I expecting for twenty-five bucks? Besides, it was better than the place where we stayed the night before—an abandoned house with boarded-up windows. We'd climbed in through a hole where a panel was busted out in the back door. Actually, come to think of it, the two places smelled about the same.

I looked around the room. There was a dresser, a TV, and two twin-sized beds separated by a little nightstand. There was paint peeling from the walls, a big yellow water stain on the ceiling, and the furniture looked shabby, like stuff that the Salvation Army might have thrown out. A few weeks before I wouldn't even have dreamed of ever setting foot in a place like this. Now I couldn't wait to put my head down on that stained bed cover.

Brent walked around the beds and opened another door. He hit the lights to reveal a bathroom.

"So, what do you think?" he said, gesturing grandly around him.

"It's a lot better than sleeping under a bridge or in some squat," Ashley commented. "Dana?"

"It doesn't look that bad," I said, trying to convince myself and Ashley and spare Brent's feelings at the same time.

"How come we could get this place for twenty-five bucks when the sign outside says thirty-nine, ninety-nine?" Ashley asked.

"That's the price for the regular people, you know, like tourists."

"Tourists?" I laughed. "Do you really think tourists would stay in a place like this?"

"Maybe really poor tourists," Brent joked. "Either way, I know the guy at the desk, and if his boss isn't around and there are rooms empty he lets people like us stay here."

"And if his boss *is* around?" I asked.

"No point in even showing up. He'd just call the cops. He thinks he's running a class place."

Ashley laughed. "If he thinks this is class, then he either has to take more medication or stop the medication he's on, because that's just delusional thinking."

"Delusional or not, his boss will be working here tomorrow morning and he won't want to see us, so we'll have to get out of here early."

"How early is early?" Ashley asked.

"Like around seven."

"Great," she said shaking her head. "This will be the first real bed I've slept in for weeks and I don't get to sleep in."

"Does your friend tell his boss that he's rented out these rooms?" I asked.

"Now you're catching on," he said, and smiled. "I think the money stays in his pocket, but what do I care? He's doing us a favour."

"If he was really doing us a favour he wouldn't charge us at all," Ashley pointed out.

"Yeah, like that's going to happen, somebody giving somebody something for nothing. Everything and everybody has a price," Brent said.

A month ago I think I might have disagreed with him. Now I wasn't so sure.

"Speaking of price, just how much money do we have left?" Brent asked.

"Let's put all our money together and count it," Ashley suggested.

Everybody emptied out their pockets, digging out the coins and bills buried in there.

"I've got seventeen dollars and twenty-eight cents," Brent said, smoothing out the bills on top of the bed and heaping the coins up with it. Of course his total included the change from the forty bucks after he'd paid for the room.

"Here's mine," Ashley added. "I've got six dollars and twenty-five . . . fifty . . . seventy-eight cents." She dropped it onto the bed on top of Brent's money. "How about you, Dana?"

"I've got around nine dollars and one subway ticket," I said as I deposited my money onto the bed as well.

"A subway ticket?" Ashley asked. "Were you really planning on actually going home?"

"Somebody gave it to me. What was I supposed to say? 'Sorry, I'm really begging for money and I don't want to take the subway'? We must have enough money for supper."

"And cigarettes," Ashley added.

I shook my head. "We'd do a lot better if we didn't waste so much money on cigarettes."

"Buying cigarettes isn't a waste," Brent said.

"It's worse than a waste. Smoking can kill you!"

Ashley laughed. "I'm still alive, and I've been smoking since I was eleven."

"Eleven . . . you're joking, right?"

She shook her head. "I can't get over the fact that you don't smoke."

Brent was sorting the money into bills and coins.

"We have a grand total of thirty-two dollars and eighty-five cents. Take some out for burgers and fries at Mickey-Dee's—oh, hey, maybe we should get the Happy Meal, kids, so we can get the toy!—and we'll still have enough left over to get us all a coffee to start tomorrow off and pick up some cigarettes."

"If we didn't buy cigarettes then we'd have enough for breakfast tomorrow, too," I said.

"You've got a point there," Brent agreed. "Let's put it to a vote. All those in favour of buying cigarettes raise your hand."

Both Brent's and Ashley's hands shot up in the air. This was one vote that I knew I could never win.

"Fine," I said. "You two can have your cigarettes. But it only seems fair that I should get something as well."

"What did you have in mind?" Brent asked.

"I get the shower first."

"You got no argument from me," Brent said.

"Me neither," Ashley agreed.

"Would *milady* care for me to run her bath for her?" Brent asked, trying his best to sound like an English butler.

"I don't want a bath. I want a shower. A long, hot shower."

"I get the shower next," Ashley said.

"In that case, maybe I should take the money and go out and get our food and bring it back here," Brent suggested as he reached down to scoop up the money.

"And you *are* going to get food, right?" Ashley asked.

I turned to face her. What did she mean by that?

"Of course," Brent said. He looked sheepish.

I wanted to ask, but I didn't. All I wanted was a shower.

"How about you get me a Big Mac meal," Ashley said.

"Same for me, but hold the pickles," I said.

"We'll make it three," he said as he stuffed the money in his pocket. "I'll be back soon, so don't take too long in the shower."

Brent started for the door.

"Brent . . . ?" Ashley called, and he stopped and turned around.

"Don't worry," he said. He opened the door and left.

"What was that all about?" I asked.

"Nothing," Ashley said. "Well, nothing much."

I gave her a questioning look.

"A couple of times Brent took our money and went to get food, but he didn't get food."

"What did he get?"

"He got stoned," she explained.

"Brent did that? That doesn't sound like him."

"It was a long time ago," she said. "Like, over a month. Besides, he doesn't even do drugs now."

"What do you mean? I've seen him smoke dope before."

"Oh, that was just marijuana. He doesn't do any *real* drugs." She paused. "I also told him if he ever did that to me again I'd make him pay . . . I told him his life was worth more than twenty bucks."

Ashley had such a hard look on her face, I knew she wasn't just joking around. Ashley was pretty tough, and I knew I never wanted to get on her bad side. A few weeks ago I would have crossed the street to walk on the other side if I'd seen her coming.

"Can I ask you something?" I began.

"Sure."

"That cop . . . he said . . . he said that he might do something worse than just arrest me if he saw me again. What did he mean?"

"He meant that he might smack you around."

"He'd do that?"

She laughed. "You sound surprised."

"But police can't just hit people."

"They're cops. They can do anything they want."

"But it's illegal to just hit somebody. It's against the law!" I protested.

She laughed louder. "You really are from the suburbs."

"What is that supposed to mean?"

"It means that the only contact you've probably had with cops is when they gave your parents a speeding ticket. It's

different down here. Cops do some things that aren't exactly by the book."

"You're telling me that all the cops downtown smack people around?" I asked.

"Not all cops," she said. "Most of them are okay, but not all of them."

"And you've seen this?"

"I've seen lots of things. Some guy doesn't do what the cops say, or maybe resists them, and then one thing leads to another."

"Have you ever been hit?"

"I've been pushed around before, but never hit. Like I said, just don't resist. If they say to move along, just move along. Don't argue, don't give them any lip or attitude, and you'll be okay."

I decided right then that no one was going to have to tell me twice. I wasn't going to give anybody any attitude. If a cop ever told me to leave, I'd just leave.

There was still one thing that nagged at me.

"The cop said that every kid on the street hooks... *everyone*."

"Not everyone," Ashley said.

"That's what I thought. I'd *never* do that!" I protested.

Ashley didn't answer right away. "You should never say never."

"I *know* I'll never hook."

Ashley gave me a look—a look of despair and anger and upset and disbelief and so many other things that I couldn't understand. "There was a time when I thought the same thing."

"Have... have you?" I asked, the words jumping out before I realized what I was saying.

She didn't answer.

"I'm . . . I'm sorry," I stammered. "I shouldn't have asked . . . it's none of my business."

"That's okay," she said. She sat there in silence, staring at the wall. "Sometimes," she said, her voice barely a whisper, "you do what you have to do . . ."

THE HOT WATER streamed down my face and body. I'd almost used up the little bar of soap scrubbing my body, trying to remove the dirt and sweat and smells that had accumulated since I'd last showered—hard to believe that was over three weeks ago. I would have felt bad about using up so much soap, but there was a second bar, sitting on the sink, that Ashley and Brent could use.

I unscrewed the top on the little container of shampoo and conditioner and smelled it; it was some sort of peachy fragrance. Not my favourite, but beggars can't be choosers, and I guess I was a real beggar now, after all. It wasn't like at home where there were a dozen different types of shampoo for different types of hair, as well as conditioners and special shower gels. Sometimes I thought my friends and I spent more time worrying about what was *on* our heads than what was *in* our heads. I wondered what Sarah and Samantha were doing right now. Probably watching TV or talking on the phone to each other or on MSN or . . . what was the point in thinking about any of that? I wondered if they thought about me the way I still thought about them. Would they have any idea at all about what was happening to me now?

I tipped the shampoo into my hand, careful to use only one-third of the bottle. I put it down and then, with both hands, worked up a lather of suds in my hair. The smell got stronger as the suds built up. I ducked my head under the stream of water and started to rinse out the soapy lather. I worked it around and around; the water pulsated through my hair against my scalp. It felt so good: the hot water massaging my head, the feel of my hair—squeaky and clean—the steam rising up, the sweet, peachy smell. I could have stayed in the shower for hours . . . that's what my mother used to say I did. She'd yell up the stairs for me to hurry or I'd be late for school. She'd even send my little sister up to pound on the door. Boy, it used to irritate me when she did that. All I wanted was to be left alone in the shower, behind the locked door, the noise of the shower blocking out all the other sounds, blocking out everything.

That was all I wanted to do now, but I couldn't. Ashley needed to take her shower, and Brent might already be back with the food. I wondered how long it would be before I got a chance to have another shower. Just then, I wouldn't even have minded my sister pounding on the door. I missed her a lot. I knew she would be confused by what I'd done—worried, upset. I wished I could have explained things to her, about why I had to leave, but I didn't, and I couldn't. I couldn't tell her. I couldn't tell anybody.

The suds cascaded down my neck and back and front and along my arms. I watched as the water and suds formed ripples as they passed over the little scars that covered my arms. I touched them with my fingers, tracing the lines. They were fading but they were still visible. Some of the marks, the deeper ones, would never fade away.

Tears came. The warm tears flowed down my cheeks and got lost in the water flowing out of the showerhead. I started to sob. My whole body got shaky and my legs felt all rubbery and weak. I slumped down to the tiled floor of the shower. I thought about my sister, and my mother, and my friends, and my school, and my room, and about how I missed every one of them—how I missed them all so much.

And then I thought about my stepfather, and the sobbing subsided and the sadness was replaced. Replaced by anger. And the searing heat of that anger dried up the tears.

chapter three

"NICE WORK."

I spun around, surprised by the voice that had called out unexpectedly from behind me. He was old—maybe in his thirties—dressed casually, not big or small, and he had a goofy-looking smile on his face. Maybe it was more of a smirk than a smile. He was by himself, which meant there were only the two of us standing underneath the bridge.

"I really like the way you've used colour," he said.

I put my hand behind my back to try to hide the can of orange spray paint I was holding. That made no sense. He'd obviously seen me working, and even if he hadn't I didn't think he could miss the twenty-five-foot-long piece of graffiti that lined the concrete wall beneath the bridge.

"You don't very often see orange and purple in the same image, but I think you've made it work." He took a couple of steps forward and I jumped back, scanning the area to the right-hand side—I could run along the concrete embankment and then get over the fence and—

"I'm not going to hurt you," he said. "Sorry if I frightened you. I'll give you some more space." He backed away a few steps and I felt an instant sense of relief—although I wasn't letting my guard down for a second. Who was this guy and why was he here and what did he want?

"I saw the start of this piece of work yesterday when I was taking the train home," he said.

"Train?" I asked.

He smiled. "Oh, good, you can talk."

I didn't answer.

"The train," he said, pointing to the tracks across the street and behind a chain-link fence and in front of some derelict buildings. "I caught sight of your image last night, and then this morning on the way in I saw you working."

I didn't like the thought of him or anybody else being able to see me.

"And I just wanted to come over to have a closer look."

"Are you a cop?" I asked.

He laughed. "Do I look like a cop?"

I didn't like it when people asked a question instead of answering the one I'd asked.

"If I were a cop, you'd be under arrest already," he said. I guess he sensed that I wanted an answer.

"If you're not a cop then what are you?"

"Maybe I'm just an art-lover on his lunch hour."

"Yeah, right, and this is an art gallery."

"It could be an art gallery, if you consider all the interesting and varied pieces of work that line the walls and buildings around here," he said.

The bridge abutments, the concrete walls of the flood-control creek, and the abandoned buildings all around here were covered in paint and chalk—words or images or markings—people trying to show their skill or maybe just to let the world know that they did really exist.

"I think if he were a young man today, Picasso would probably be exploring street images."

"Picasso?"

"A very famous artist. Have you heard of him?"

I snorted. "Pablo Picasso, born on October 25, 1881, in Spain."

I'd done a project on Picasso for art class last term. He was one of my favourite painters. I loved his abstract vision and the way he used colours. Anybody could paint something the way it actually looked, but he could create a whole new way of seeing things.

"I'm impressed," he said.

"Everybody's heard of Picasso."

"Strange as it sounds, some people haven't. And most of those who do certainly don't know his birthday. Did you know that initially his work was dismissed by the art establishment of the day?"

I knew that. I knew lots. But as far as I could tell this conversation was going nowhere fast. Time to get to the point.

"So what's Picasso got to do with *this*?" I asked, pointing at my work on the concrete wall.

"I don't believe he ever did any of his work using a spray can on concrete, but there is an abstract quality to your work. I particularly like that figure on the far left . . . excellent."

"Thanks," I mumbled. That was actually *my* favourite part of the whole thing . . . no . . . my favourite part was just doing the whole thing. There was something about drawing or painting that just freed my mind up, helped me to escape from the world. Right now it was the only escape I had. It made me feel peaceful. Even though the images I was painting weren't of hearts and flowers and little birdies in trees—more like jagged lines and clashing colours and weird faces—it made me feel good to lay them down. I think Brent and Ashley would have come with me if I'd asked, but I felt pretty safe here on my own. Come to think of it now, though, maybe ditching my friends wasn't such a great idea.

"Do you know the major difference between your work and that of Picasso?" he asked.

I didn't answer. What sort of a question was that?

"Picasso never got arrested for expressing his artistic vision," he said.

I felt a rush of fear—he was a cop and he was going to arrest me and—

"Don't worry," he said, reading my expression. "I'm not a cop. Do I really look like one?" he asked again.

"Cops can look like anything," I said. I thought about what Ashley had said about some cops roughing people up.

"I guess they could. I just know that if I saw you working down here, somebody else might have seen your work . . . somebody who doesn't have the same appreciation I do for art. What some people see as art, other people see as vandalism. You might want to think about that. How much longer is it going to take you to finish?" he asked.

"I don't know . . . not long."

"Then don't let me disturb you. I'll stop bothering you and you can get back to work. I'll just go and sit right over there." He walked over to a cement pillar, wiped it off with his hand, and took a seat.

He was staring intently at the painting, like he was studying it. I watched him closely while he looked at the painting. Who was this guy and why was he here and—?

"Could I ask you one more question?" he said.

I didn't answer, which he took to mean yes.

"Why, specifically, did you choose to use those two colours together?"

"I thought you liked orange and purple."

"Oh, I do, I was just wondering what led you to make that bold artistic statement."

I shrugged. "Those were the colours I found in the dumpster behind the hardware store."

He laughed. "Would you mind if I came back this evening and took some pictures of your work?"

"You want to take pictures of this?" I was having real trouble taking this guy seriously.

"Definitely. If I don't, it will be lost forever. How long do you think it will be before they cover it over with grey paint? I guess that's the other major difference between a street artist and Picasso. City workers never went around and painted over his masterpieces. So, would you mind?"

"I don't care . . . it's a free world."

"We like to think it is," he said. "I was wondering, are you self-taught or do you have some special training in art?"

Despite myself, I laughed. "I don't think anybody teaches people how to do this."

"Not that, specifically," he agreed. "But art in general. Have you taken courses?"

"I've taken classes in drawing, and I went to art camp last summer." I'd always dreamed about being an artist.

"Last summer . . . so I assume you've been on the streets less than a year."

"What makes you think I'm on the streets?" I asked.

"Just guessing. People with homes don't generally do a lot of dumpster-diving. You said that's where you got the spray paint."

"That doesn't mean I'm living on the streets," I pointed out.

"No, that's true. But consider this clue: you still have the purple paint from yesterday's work on your hands."

I looked down. He was right, there were streaks of purple paint.

"I think that most people who had a place to go would have washed that off when they got home last night."

"What makes you think I didn't use purple today?" I asked.

"You didn't," he said, shaking his head. "The purple was on yesterday."

He was right, which shocked me. How could he tell that as he passed by on a train?

"So, how long have you been living on the streets?"

I didn't answer.

"I have something for you," he said as he stood up.

"I don't want anything from you!" I snapped. "Back off!" And I held the can of spray paint out in front of me like a weapon.

He held up his hands like he was surrendering.

"I have no desire to be part of your next creation. Orange is not my colour."

He lowered his hands slowly, reached into his pocket, and pulled something out. "I'm going to leave this right here," he said as he bent down. "This is my business card." He reached over and put a rock on top of it so it wouldn't blow away, then backed off. "I work for a drop-in centre. But if you need a meal or a place to have a shower, don't bother coming."

"What did you say?" I asked, not believing my ears.

"I said we're not a place where you can get a meal or get washed up or sleep, although we can help make arrangements for all of those. We're a different type of drop-in centre."

A useless type of drop-in centre was what I wanted to say, but I didn't.

"What we offer involves art. We're a place where you can get materials, things like paint and canvas, or clay and a potter's wheel, to use some of that talent you obviously have. The address is on the card. Maybe we'll see you some time."

He started to walk away and then stopped and turned around. "Ask on the street and people will tell you that the centre is legit. Just ask around."

He started to walk away a second time and then stopped again. "My name is on the card. I'm Robert Erickson. Who are you?"

I didn't answer. That was none of his business.

"Okay, be careful. Maybe we'll see you at the centre some time."

He gave a wave and started up the embankment again.

"Hey!" I called out.

He turned around.

"It's Dana."

He nodded his head. "Okay, Dana, maybe we'll see you around. And I really do like what you've created here. You have some real talent."

chapter four

THE CAT RUBBED UP against my legs. It was a beaten-up old orange cat, thin, its tail bent at the end, and it was missing the very top of one ear. Living on the streets had taken its toll on her.

"You're a nice girl, aren't you?" I said.

She rose up on her back legs and I reached out to pet her. She pressed against my hands as I scratched behind her ears and she made a noise—a strange sort of noise. I bent down lower to hear. It was sort of a raspy, uneven sound, but it was unmistakable—she was trying to purr. I shook my head. All beaten up, a stray living in the back alleys of the city, and she was still happy because I was showing her a little affection, a little caring. I didn't know if that was wonderful or sad, or both.

"Maybe I have something for you," I said. I reached deep into my pocket and pulled out a package of Chicken McNuggets. There were three nuggets left over from supper the night before. I'd been planning to have them as a bedtime snack but I'd forgotten. I pulled one out of the package.

"I think I can afford to share one with you. Here you go."

She snatched it from my hand, her little sharp teeth scraping against my fingers. It dropped to the ground and she gulped it down hungrily.

"You're even more hungry than I am, aren't you, girl?" I looked at the two remaining nuggets. The cat needed them more than I did. Besides, they didn't look too appealing. I dropped them to the ground. She grabbed a second nugget, chewed it a couple of times, and then swallowed it down. The third was gone in seconds.

The cat looked up at me.

"That's all I've got," I said. "Sorry."

She began rubbing up against me again. It felt good.

"I don't have anything more . . . but maybe I can bring you something some other time."

She looked as though she understood what I was saying.

"Hey, Dana!"

At the sound of Brent's voice I jumped up, and the cat scrambled away.

"There you are," he said. He and Ashley were standing at the end of the alley, and they were both carrying newspapers . . . lots of newspapers.

"We couldn't see you at first," he said.

"Was that a cat?" Ashley asked.

"I was feeding it."

"That's not too bright," Brent told me.

"Hey, it was hungry!"

"Every mangy, stray cat in the whole city is hungry," he said. "Who knows what disease it might have? You've got to think about yourself. Besides, aren't *you* hungry?"

"Not really . . . not that hungry."

"Good. Then once we sell these newspapers I can have your breakfast as well as mine."

"We're going to sell papers?"

"Yeah, what did you think we were going to do with all of these?"

I shrugged. "Where'd they come from?"

"We liberated them," Brent said.

"We set them free," Ashley added, and chuckled.

"They were locked up, imprisoned really, inside a newspaper box. We just opened up the door and let them escape."

"You bought them?" That didn't make sense.

"We bought *one*," Brent said. "We put in fifty cents to open up the box and then we took out all the papers that were in there."

"All forty-three papers," Ashley said.

"You stole them?"

"Don't sound so shocked," Ashley said.

"I'm not shocked . . . not *that* shocked."

Brent shrugged. "Haven't you ever stolen anything in your whole life?"

"I've stolen things before," I lied.

"You have? Like what?" Ashley asked.

"Stuff," I said, unable to come up with a more specific lie.

Ashley laughed. "Stuff . . . yeah, right. You probably didn't have enough time to steal anything because you were too busy taking piano lessons and tap-dancing classes."

"Actually, it was jazz and hip hop," I answered sheepishly.

"Ooh, hip hop, now that *really* makes you street!"

"Give her a break, Ash," Brent said.

"That's okay," I said. "I guess she's right."

"Of course I'm right. And that's why the two of us have to take care of you."

"And besides," Brent said, "we didn't steal those papers, we *liberated* them . . . weren't you listening? When we opened the door all those poor newspapers just jumped out into our arms. Isn't that how it happened?" he asked Ashley.

"That's how I remember it. Can you take some of these?" she asked.

I took a dozen or so off the top of the pile in her arms. "So what do we do now?"

"We find a place to sell them. Forty papers at fifty cents each comes out to twenty bucks," Brent said. "Breakfast and cigarette money."

"It would be great if we could get enough money to get a motel room again," I said.

"That would be nice," Ashley agreed.

"Nice, but probably not going to happen," Brent said. "Let's just sell the papers and take it from there."

"Where are we going to sell them?"

"Down by one of the off-ramps coming off the expressway," he explained.

"Let's go," Ashley said. "If we really want to try to get a room tonight we need to sell all the papers and then do some serious panhandling after that."

I took one more look down the alley. The cat was peeking out from behind a dumpster. I'd be back later.

THE LIGHT TURNED RED and the cars started to slow down and stop on the ramp. Brent and Ashley walked between the two rows of vehicles, offering papers to the drivers. A car window slid down and Ashley handed the guy a paper and took his money.

We were taking turns going out to sell, and it was my turn to sit on the stack of remaining papers, which was getting smaller all the time.

The light changed and the cars started off again. Brent and Ashley skipped through the cars and reached the safety of the sidewalk on the far side. We were separated by the stream of traffic—cars and trucks racing off the highway, trying to make it off the ramp and onto the street before the light changed to red again.

I looked off to the side. There were two people coming toward me, a girl and a guy, and they had a dog with them. It was a big, black retriever with a red bandana tied around its neck. Neither of them looked much older than me. As they got closer I could also see that they were street.

"May I pet your dog?" I asked.

"No problem," the girl said.

I reached over and gave the dog a scratch behind the ears. It turned and started to sniff me.

"Probably smells cat," I said.

"You have a cat?" she asked.

"No, not really, but I was petting one just a while ago. What's your dog's name?"

"Squat."

"We called him that because that's where we found him . . . in a squat," the boy explained.

"Yeah. You should have seen him, nothing but skin and bones," the girl said.

"It looks like he's been eating pretty good since then," I said. The dog was actually a bit fat.

"That was months ago. We make sure he eats," the boy said.

"He eats, even if we don't eat," she added, a bit proudly. "Some people may think that's stupid but—"

"I don't think it's stupid!" I said, jumping in. "That's just right. He's your pet and you have a responsibility to take care of him, and that's what you're doing."

"Exactly."

A car horn sounded and I looked up in time to see Brent and Ashley dodging traffic as they came across the road.

"How's it going?" Brent asked.

"Good, man . . . good to see you," the boy said as he and Brent shook hands. The girl gave Brent a hug and then hugged Ashley. Obviously they all knew each other already.

"This is our friend, Dana," Brent said.

"Hi, I'm Spencer, and this is my lady, Anna . . . and you've met Squat already."

"How you doing, Squat?" Ashley asked as she gave the dog a hug around the neck. "I love his bandana."

Anna smiled. "Nothing's too fine for our baby."

"Where you staying these days?" Brent asked.

"Warehouse just south of Queen Street," Spencer told him. "I think it used to be a shoe factory."

"I know the one," Brent said.

"Any space there?" Ashley asked.

"Big place," Anna said. "Not much privacy and lots of people there every night."

"Is it safe?" Ashley asked.

"It's safe for us," Spencer said. "Nobody's going to mess with us as long as Squat's with us."

"But he seems so gentle," I said.

"He is gentle," Anna said, "unless somebody bothers us."

"Watch," Spencer said. "Squat!" he ordered. "Defend!"

The dog bared his teeth and started to growl. I jumped away, as did Ashley and Brent.

"Down, boy," Spencer said, and instantly the dog was silent, and he started to wag his tail.

"Any luck with the papers?" Anna asked.

"It'll make us enough to eat," Ashley answered.

"Speaking of which, we'd better get going if we're going to get some food today," Spencer said. "Maybe we'll see you later. Come and crash with us tonight."

"Maybe we'll do that," Brent said. "Take it easy."

The three of them walked away.

As soon as they were out of earshot, Brent turned to me. "You have to be more careful," he said. He actually sounded kind of ticked off.

"Anna and Spencer? But they seem nice."

"They are nice, but you didn't know them," Brent said.

"But *you* knew them."

"Yeah, but you were talking to them before you knew that. I know lots of people, but that doesn't mean they're all nice. There's some pretty dangerous people out here on the street."

"And some of the most dangerous people are the ones who don't even look dangerous," Ashley added. "That's what makes them so dangerous. You'd know that if you'd been around more. You learn who's safe and who's not safe . . . and sometimes you have to learn it the hard way."

"Look, Dana, there are a lot of bad people out here," Brent went on. "Most of the people on the street are no different from you and me and Ashley . . . they're just trying to do what they have to do to survive, trying not to hurt anybody else. But other people don't care what they have to do to survive. If they need to hurt you, they'll do it."

"Some of them actually seem to enjoy it," Ashley said. "Some people like causing other people pain, you know."

That made me remember the pervert who had got me in trouble with the police. He'd looked like a nice enough guy.

"Maybe we should get a dog like Squat," I suggested.

"It's not worth it. Besides, they don't really have the dog for protection."

"They don't?"

Brent shook his head. "They have the dog so they can take care of it. It's more like their baby than their pet."

"He's right," Ashley agreed. "And I guess it's better to have a dog out here than a kid."

"Nobody would have a kid," I said.

"You think because you live on the street that you can't get pregnant and have a baby?" Brent asked.

"No, I just can't imagine anybody living out here with a baby. There's no way you could raise a kid out here."

"I've seen it," Ashley said. "Although they don't keep the kid for long. The police and the child welfare people come and take the baby away. It goes into foster care."

"That would at least be better than living out here," I said.

"Obviously you've never been in a foster home," Ashley muttered.

I looked at Ashley. Had she . . . ?

"I've been in a few," she said, in answer to my unasked question. "And a couple were the kinds of places they should have been taking kids away from. Although a couple were pretty good . . . better than living with my mother."

Ashley didn't talk a whole lot about her family or her past. I wondered if maybe she was going to open up about it now.

"Let's not talk about it any more," she said, abruptly.

"I agree," Brent added. "No more talk about foster homes or getting a dog. Anyway, I already have two pets," he said.

"You do?"

Brent smiled. "Yeah . . . their names are Ashley and Dana . . . and it's enough work taking care of them. Now, are we going to finish selling these newspapers or what?"

"We'll sell this time," I said. "How about if you take a seat here and watch the papers and Ashley and I will go out and do the dirty work."

"Sounds like a plan."

"OKAY, LET'S SEE WHAT WE'VE GOT," Ashley said.

We started emptying our pockets onto the picnic table. Along with selling all the papers we'd also done some panhandling.

"I don't think we have enough for a room," Brent said.

"We only need twenty-five bucks," I pointed out.

"We need at least forty if we're going to eat and have cigarettes, too," Ashley said.

"And I wouldn't mind buying a couple of joints," Brent added.

I wanted to say something, but didn't.

Brent started to go through the bills and coins we'd dumped on the table. It was obvious there wasn't going to be enough. Maybe if we saved some of the money from today and got more money tomorrow we could get a place the next night.

"What's this?" Brent asked as he picked up a card—the business card from that guy that I'd stuffed in my pocket and then forgotten about. It had been tangled up with the change I'd pulled out of my pocket.

I reached out and took it from him. "It's nothing . . . just something some guy gave me."

"What sort of guy?" Ashley asked.

"A street worker guy. He wanted to know if I wanted to go to some drop-in centre."

"Which one?" Brent asked. "I think I've been to every one in the city."

I looked at the card. Under his name it said the name of the centre. "It's called Sketches," I said. "Have you been to that one?"

He shook his head. "Never been, but I've heard of it."

"He said it was like an art drop-in centre."

"What does that mean?" Ashley asked.

"He said it's where people can go if they want to do some art."

"Why would people want to do that?" Ashley questioned.

"Lots of people like doing art stuff," I protested.

"Sounds like something you'd do."

"He saw me spray-painting the wall under the bridge by the tracks," I explained. "He said it was good."

"So, did you take art lessons before or after your hip hop classes?" Ashley asked, with a smirk.

"Before *and* after. I took art lessons for years," I said. I didn't care if she did make fun of me. "I like art. It was my favourite subject in school. I was good at it."

"Mine was lunch," Brent chipped in. "And I was *really* good at it."

"So you're thinking of going there, to that drop-in centre?" Ashley asked.

"I was thinking about it . . . maybe."

"I know it. It's over on King Street, close to Bathurst," Brent said. "They have a storefront sort of place."

"And it's legit, right?" I asked Brent.

He shrugged. "Must be . . . the guy has cards. Now how about getting back to the important stuff. We don't have enough for a motel room."

"Could we stay at that place where Spencer and Anna and Squat are staying?" I asked.

"I don't think so," Brent said.

"Why not?"

"There are lots of people staying there."

"But he also said there was lots of *space*."

"Doesn't matter how much space there is. The more people there are, the more chance some of those people won't be good people. Besides, a crowd attracts police, and it's best that we stay away from them as well."

After my encounter with that cop I wasn't going to argue with him. "So where will we sleep?"

"Don't worry. I know hundreds of places."

I believed that, but I was still going to worry.

chapter five

I STOPPED ON the opposite side of the street, directly across from the drop-in centre. In big, bright, colourful letters it said "SKETCHES." There were some kids standing out front, leaning against the glass, talking, and some were having a smoke. They were the sort of people who I would have crossed the street to avoid if I'd seen them coming toward me a month ago. Now I was still cautious, but I'd learned not to be afraid. Or at least not to look like I was afraid. Showing fear was the worst thing you could do. You had to look cool, in control, like you belonged there. Brent and Ashley knew how to do it. They had the look, and the walk—the saunter.

I tried to look around the passing cars and trucks and buses to see through the window of the storefront. The sun glaring off the glass made that impossible. All I saw was a reflection of the activity on the street. Either I had to get closer or just stop wasting my time and leave—but leave for where? To join Ash and Brent killing time on Yonge Street?

I waited for a break in the traffic and then crossed, dodging the cars. I skipped up onto the sidewalk and stopped. I didn't know if I should go in. I didn't know who was there or what they'd say. I felt my gut get all tight.

Part of me wanted to just take off, leave, go, but a bigger part wanted to go through the door and find out what was inside. I reached into my pocket and pulled out the crumpled card. I unfolded it and tried to smooth it out. I guess it was sort of like my invitation to go in. And I realized that that was what I really wanted to do. Most of what we did every day we did to survive, to get enough money to eat and a place out of the wet or wind or cold nights. There was hardly anything I did that made a difference or made me feel like I was somebody. Painting that concrete wall with those spray cans was the closest I'd felt to that. Maybe here I could do more.

The kids standing in front of the place ignored me as I walked by. I stopped at the front door. There was a sign: "Sketches is a working studio for street-involved, homeless, at-risk youth. This is a drug-free, violence-free, feel free to play space." That sounded good to me. I opened the door and was startled by the loud *ping* of a bell. The music I could hear from the outside was a lot louder inside. It was a band I knew but didn't really like.

Carefully I looked around. There were maybe ten or twelve people. Everybody looked older than me, but nobody much older. It was also pretty obvious that everybody looked street . . . piercings, tattoos, clothes. I suddenly felt like a kid from the suburbs again, not sure of myself, not sure that I should be there. I wished I looked tougher, but who was I kidding? I didn't look or feel tough at all.

Four kids were sitting on some broken-down old couches. They were munching on some apples and talking and laughing. Three others were standing in front of canvases, painting.

"Hello! How are you?"

I spun around. It was a woman. She had a big smile on her face and her hair was all spiked and shooting up into the air in a dozen directions. She was wearing a large white T-shirt that was covered in splotches of a dozen different colours of paint.

"I'm fine, I guess," I answered.

"Welcome to Sketches."

"Thanks."

"My name is Nicki. I'm the director of this program." She reached out her hand and I awkwardly shook it. "And you are . . . ?" she asked.

"I'm Carolyn," I lied. Carolyn was my mother's name, and it was the first one that popped into my head.

"Is this your first time here?" she asked.

"Yeah, my first time." At least that wasn't a lie.

"It's great to have you here."

That was something I hadn't been hearing too often from people these days. Mostly they were just happy for me to be somewhere else. People in stores, people in their cars, cops, people walking on the street—they all wanted me to go away. That is, those that didn't just pretended I wasn't there.

"So how did you hear about our program?" Nicki asked.

I held the card out and she took it.

"He saw me doing some painting . . . under a bridge."

"Under a bridge . . . were you using a lot of purples and oranges?"

"Uh, yeah, I was," I admitted, wondering how she'd know that.

She furrowed her brow. "Robert told me about you, but I thought he said your name was something different."

I swallowed hard. "I might have told him I was Dana," I admitted. "Sometimes people call me Dana."

"That's a nice name," she said. "Would you rather we called you Carolyn or Dana?"

"It doesn't matter . . . whatever you want."

"No, it does matter. It's about what *you* want."

"I guess Dana would be okay."

"Then Dana is what it'll be. I really like your work, Dana."

"You saw it?"

"Very vivid, bold—exciting. I'm only sorry I didn't get to see the original."

"What do you mean?"

"I only saw the photographs Robert took."

"That's right, he said he was going to do that."

"And it's a good thing he did because the original has already been destroyed," Nicki said.

"It has?"

"The city doesn't care if it's a beautiful work of art or a scrawl and some swear words, they just cover it up with grey paint."

Damn. I'd known it wasn't going to be there forever, but somehow I'd hoped it would last longer.

"When did they do it?" I asked.

"A few days ago. I'm sorry."

That seemed so typical. The good things never lasted.

"Just bad timing. The city maintenance crews were working in that area," she said. "So, would you like a tour?"

"Sure, I guess," I said, although there really didn't seem to be that much to see.

"This," she said, spreading her arms and motioning around us, "is our main studio. This is the place where our clients have a chance to work in visual arts. This studio is dedicated to painting in a variety of media, including watercolours, oils, acrylics—"

"I like acrylics," I said.

"It sounds like you've had some experience."

"My mother . . . she enrolled me in all kinds of art lessons."

"It sounds like she appreciated your artistic side," Nicki said.

"Yeah she did." It felt strange to talk about my mother. It felt strange to even think about her. I wondered what she was doing right now, what my sister was doing. Were they thinking of me? Were they worried about me?

"Come on and I'll show you the other studios," Nicki said.

"There are others?"

"Just follow me."

As we walked past one of the painters, she reached out and put an arm around the girl's shoulders.

"That is really beautiful," Nicki said.

"It's nothing, really," the girl replied.

"It's *something*, something to be proud of!"

"It's really not that good. I think—"

"I think you're forgetting something really important," Nicki said, taking the girl's hand.

The girl nodded her head and a slight smile came to her lips. "Thank you," she said. "It is pretty good."

"Almost as good as the person who made it." Nicki gave the girl a big hug and she broke into a huge grin.

We walked away and Nicki turned back toward me.

"Hardest thing around here isn't to help people to create beautiful art, but to convince them that they have created it. Can you imagine somebody not liking that painting?" she asked.

"It was good," I agreed.

We walked through a door and into another room. The music on one side of the door was replaced by music on the other—this time more metallic and blaring. The room was filled with workbenches, and tools lined the walls. There was one guy in the room.

"This is our industrial arts studio. He's creating and customizing gas-powered scooters!" she yelled over the music.

The guy looked over at us, waved, and gave a goofy smile. He had thick glasses, hair that shot up in a thousand different directions, and he looked as though he ought to be in the audiovisual club at school. Compared to him I looked downright street. He turned back to his work.

We moved through another door. I was both impressed and amazed to discover how much of the music was blocked out when she closed the door behind us. We were now standing in a room that held desks and computers. There was nobody else there.

"Although you can't tell right now, this is one of our most popular studios. In here people are being instructed in how to design and create websites. We have people doing some amazing stuff. There's a chance, and it's still in the initial stages, that a few of our participants are going to create their own online zine. Isn't that exciting?"

"Yeah, I guess it is."

"By the way, are you hungry?" Nicki asked.

"I'm okay," I said.

"You are?" She made it sound as though she didn't believe me. "What have you had to eat today?"

"Well . . . I had a coffee . . . and a doughnut," I said.

"Then you must be hungry. And even if you're not, I am. Come and join me for a bite to eat."

We went through another door and were in a room with tables and chairs and a fridge and stove and a toaster on the counter. The counter and sink were piled high with dirty dishes.

Nicki picked up a knife off the counter and wiped the blade on a cloth. She took a bagel from a basket and carefully sliced it in two.

"Do you want one too?" she asked.

They did look good. "That would be okay . . . sure . . . thanks."

"Do you want it toasted?"

"Yes, please."

She took a second bagel, cut it in two, and then popped all four halves into the toaster.

"We have juice, too. Apple and orange."

"Could I have an orange juice?" I'd been craving fresh juice or some fruit or something that didn't come from a fast-food place.

"Help yourself." She pointed to the fridge in the corner of the room.

When I opened it up, it was almost empty, but the bottom shelf was filled with little plastic juice containers. I grabbed an orange juice.

"It really isn't our mandate to feed people, but we have some contacts—nice people in the community—who donate food."

I sat down on one of the chairs around the table, and she took the seat right across from me.

"So, tell me what you know about Sketches," she said.

"I don't really know much," I said, shaking my head. "Just what you showed me today."

"In some ways, what you see is what you get around here. We've been operating an art drop-in centre for the past four years. Our goal is to allow street-involved and homeless youth a place to go to express themselves through art."

"You mean people just drop in and do art?" I asked.

"Five days a week our doors are open to allow people to do just that," Nicki said.

"And I can do that if I want?"

"If that's what you want to do. As well as the daily drop-ins, though, we also have special programs, classes, where peers and community artists come in and give instruction on specific techniques to help you become a better artist."

"It sounds sort of like school," I said.

"Not like any school I ever went to, but we will help you to learn new things. Anyway, you're free to just come and use our studios and materials to create and explore your artistic vision, if that's what you want," she said.

"And what do you want from me?" I asked.

"Nothing. Although we do have expectations of our participants."

"What sort of expectations?" I asked suspiciously.

"Nothing too unusual. We ask that people who attend our program respect the place and the people who use it. We all know that lots of bad things happen on the street," she continued. "We just want them to stay out there and not be brought in through our front door. While you're in here, we insist that people treat *you* with respect and caring, and we expect *you* to act the same way. The street may be just outside our door, but it stays out there. There are absolutely no weapons or violence or drugs bought or sold or used while you're here. Can you live up to that?"

"Sure." That wouldn't be hard.

"Good. We like to think of this as a sanctuary. People can't be safe to pursue their art if they're not feeling safe to begin with."

That did sound good . . . maybe too good to be true.

"Would you like to start today?" Nicki asked.

I shook my head. "I'd like to . . . but . . . but I have to get going. I'm meeting some people, some friends. Maybe I'll come back tomorrow or the next day." That morning I hadn't even been sure I was going to walk in the door. I figured I'd had enough for one day. Besides, I really was supposed to meet up with Brent and Ashley at another subway station to hustle more change.

"Any day is fine, but if you can't come for a while we understand. Sometimes it takes a lot of time and effort to get the things you need to survive on the street. Do you have a place to stay tonight?"

"I have a place," I said. I knew Ashley and Brent would take care of that.

"Because if you do need a place I can arrange something."

"I've got a place," I repeated.

"A shelter or a squat?" she asked.

I didn't answer. I didn't know where we were staying, but even if I had known I didn't think I'd tell her. It wasn't any of her business, really.

"That's okay," Nicki said. "You don't have to answer any questions if you don't want to. We're not cops or caseworkers.

We're just here to help you explore your art and help you—if you want our help. Does that sound fair?"

I nodded.

"Good."

Nicki got up and walked over to the counter. The bagels had popped up. She took them from the toaster, put the four halves on a paper plate, and began buttering them.

"I'm actually not that hungry," she said. "It's a shame to let good food go to waste. How about if you eat them both?"

She offered me the plate. I hesitated.

"Come on, don't be stubborn. If you're not that hungry yourself you can take them with you—and a few more juices—for you or your friends. And there are some muffins. They're a day old, but they're still good . . . take some of those, as well."

My instant reaction was to say no, to not take them, but I was hungry. And even if I wasn't, maybe Ashley or Brent would want them.

"Thanks," I said. I took the plate.

"I've got to get back out to the studio," Nicki said. "I'll see you tomorrow . . . or whenever you want to come back. Take care, and it was nice to meet you."

Part of me wanted to follow her out to the studio. Instead I took a big bite of the bagel. It tasted good. Maybe the bagel wouldn't be the only thing that was good here. Maybe. Maybe not.

chapter six

"WE'LL JUST MAKE THIS A LITTLE BIT WIDER," Brent said. He gave it a sharp kick and the board splintered into three pieces. "Did they really think that was going to keep anybody out?"

He reached down and grabbed the pieces, twisting and yanking, the nails squealing as he worked to pull the boards free of the window frame. He took the pieces of wood and tossed them away, then bent down and crawled in through the window, disappearing into the darkness inside. Suddenly there was light, and Brent reappeared holding a flashlight.

"Where did you get that?" Ashley asked.

"I got it at that Wal-Mart store—special five-finger discount. Watch yourselves when you're crawling in. There's some broken glass." He aimed the light at the little shards of glass still clinging to the edges of the frame.

Ashley dropped to her knees and crawled in after him. I turned and looked around. I couldn't see anybody or anything except the dark outlines of the abandoned buildings that surrounded us, but I still imagined there were eyes on us.

I couldn't help but wonder what sort of place Nicki had had in mind when she'd offered to find me somewhere for the night. It couldn't have been any worse than crawling in through the broken window of an abandoned building.

"You waiting for a formal invitation?" Brent asked.

I got down on my knees and crawled in after them, careful to avoid the broken glass. Once inside I got back on my feet. Brent shone the light around the building. It was some sort of old factory or warehouse. It was empty, and the ceiling soared high over our heads.

"You ever been in this place before?" Ashley asked Brent.

"I've been in *every* place before."

"So you know your way around in here?" I asked.

"I said I'd been here, not that I memorized the floor plan. Just follow me."

I stayed close to Brent, just a few steps behind the beam of light he projected in front of himself. Aside from that little light, the building was pitch-black. The space was so big that I couldn't see the ceiling or the walls, and there was no way of telling what else—or who else—was there. Under my feet, I could feel and hear pieces of glass on the crumbling, uneven concrete.

I hated being in a new squat, but there was no choice tonight. We'd shown up at the building we'd slept in for most of the past week to find the door boarded up and a guard in a security car sitting in the alley. If we had tried to break in we would have been arrested. The guard would probably be there for a few nights before they sent him off to watch something else. That was the way it worked. Whoever owned these abandoned buildings didn't really want us to trespass, but they didn't want to spend much money to make sure nobody ever did it, either. Instead it was like there was some sort of agreement between all the street kids and all the owners that we could sleep in one place for a few days before we were chased off and had to stay someplace else.

"This looks encouraging," Brent said as he shone the light down a small hallway. We trailed behind him along the corridor. It led to a number of smaller rooms—offices.

"Wooden floors," Brent said, shining his light downward. He pressed his foot against the floor and it creaked. "It's always better to sleep on wood than concrete. How about if we sleep here?"

"Looks like somebody *has* been sleeping here," Ashley pointed out.

Brent shone the light around the room. There were newspapers and blankets and bits of clothing scattered around. He walked over and grabbed one of the papers and studied it under the light of his flashlight.

"It's old . . . months old . . . I can hardly read it, but the date on it is way back in April."

"Just because that one's old doesn't mean that there aren't some newer ones. Maybe the person is even coming back tonight," I said.

"Maybe, but if he does he's going to find he's short a couple of blankets." Brent reached down and grabbed one of the blankets that littered the floor.

"Do you really want to do that?" I asked.

"I guess I do."

He walked out of the room and we trailed behind him into a larger office. In the light I could see a couple of broken-down old desks that had been shoved up against the wall.

Brent went over and sat down on one of the desks. Ashley sat down beside him. "Not quite twin beds," he said, "but I think we've found where we're crashing tonight,"

"Not quite," I agreed. "But I do like being up off the floor."

"Too bad somebody didn't throw forty bucks at you today," Brent joked.

"Couldn't we just go and sleep outside tonight?" I suggested. Sometimes we slept in the park. It wasn't bad to lie on the grass and look up at the stars. "It's almost like we're camping."

"Sounds like she'd like Tent Town," Ashley said.

"Tent Town?" I asked.

"It's a place where a whole bunch of homeless people have set up tents," Brent explained. "Not the worst place . . . if you have one. Do you happen to have a tent on you?" he asked.

"We could still sleep outside," I insisted.

"Not tonight. It looks like it's going to rain. Don't worry, we're safer in here than we would be out there," Brent said.

"I guess you're right."

Being outside meant that anybody—other kids, bums, even cops—could come by at any moment. It might mean getting moved along or arrested, or robbed and roughed up. I just didn't like being all closed in like this, inside of a big, old, creepy building. Outside I could run. Here I was trapped by the walls and ceiling and the memories of whatever this building used to be.

"How about if we eat?" Ashley asked.

"Suits me. I'm starving," Brent said.

"Me too."

"Didn't they feed you at that drop-in centre?" Ashley asked.

"I had some juice and a toasted bagel . . . two toasted bagels." I didn't mention the muffins. I'd walked away with three but had eaten them before I met up with Brent and Ashley. I felt bad, like I had sort of cheated them. No, it wasn't like I had *sort of* cheated them—I *had* cheated them. I wouldn't do that again, even if I was starving.

"I hope those bagels didn't spoil your appetite," Ashley said.

"I'm really hungry. What do you have?"

Ashley took her pack off her back and undid the zipper. She pulled out a white bag.

"We can have four each," she said.

"Four of what each?" I asked.

She pulled out a box of doughnuts. Ugh! I never would have believed I could get sick of doughnuts, but they were cheap—and even cheaper when you grabbed the day-olds from the dumpster—and some days it seemed like we were eating nothing else.

"That's all the money we had left after buying some more cigarettes," Brent explained.

"It's hard when there's *three* of us eating and only *two* of us are hustling the spare change," Ashley said, sounding annoyed.

"Sorry."

"I thought you were just going to drop in to that place for a minute or two and leave," Ashley said. "You were there for a couple of hours."

I hadn't meant to stay, but on my way out I'd started talking to this girl who was painting, and then one thing had led to another.

"What were you doing all that time?" Ashley demanded.

"I was working with acrylics . . . painting."

"I know what acrylics are," Ashley said. "It's just that while we were working, you were playing."

"Cut her some slack," Brent said. "She was just having some fun."

"We all have to work if we all want to eat," Ashley pointed out.

"Eating is important," Brent agreed. "But just because this isn't something that interests you or me doesn't mean it isn't important to her." He turned to me. "And painting makes you happy, right?"

I nodded. And I realized then that he was right—that an hour or so at the drop-in had made me happier than I'd felt in a very long time.

"Then you should go there sometimes," Brent said firmly, as though this were his official decision. "We all know that finding a little happiness out here isn't the easiest thing in the world."

MY EYES POPPED OPEN and for a split second I didn't know where I was and I was scared. Then it came back. I was in the abandoned building, sleeping on top of two desks pushed together against the wall. Ashley was beside me, and Brent was beside her on the outside. He was always on the outside. He made sure he was always between us and whatever could hurt us . . . and there were so many things.

My ears perked up. I heard something moving around in the darkness. I slowly sat up and peered over Ashley and Brent into the darkness. I couldn't see anything, but I could still hear it. There was somebody moving around in the room. I felt a rush of panic. I heard more rustling . . . not loud. Carefully, slowly, I reached to the place where I remembered that Brent had left the flashlight. I fumbled around until I found it. I turned it on and shone the light around the room and—a big brown rat sat up, its red eyes gleaming back at me! A shudder shot up my spine. The rat raced away from the light. I could hear it even after it had disappeared from sight.

I wanted to wake up Brent and Ashley and tell them about the rat . . . but what was the point? It wasn't like they didn't know there were rats in the world. It wasn't like we hadn't seen rats before. It seemed as though there were rats everywhere in this city, but that still didn't make me feel any less spooked by the appearance of this one.

I lay back down. I didn't know if I'd be able to get back to sleep but I had to try. I clutched the flashlight tightly against my chest, holding it like a shield or a sword. I focused the beam of light up onto the ceiling above my head and moved it around. That was what I used to do in my bedroom when I was little—shine a flashlight up onto the ceiling and make it dance all around. The beam would reflect off the little stars and moons that my mother had stuck onto the ceiling, shining green in the darkness. Here there were no stars or moons. There was just peeling paint and water stains.

I turned off the flashlight and the room became thick with darkness again. Maybe it was better not to look. Seeing bad things coming didn't stop them from coming, and there were lots of things in the world that were worse than rats. Lots of things. At least I was safe from some of those other things here.

chapter seven

I PEELED BACK the little opening on the plastic coffee lid and took a sip. It was hot and it tasted really good. I took another sip, a bigger one this time.

I was never allowed coffee at home. My mother thought I was too young to drink it. Funny how you can be too young for something but old enough for something else altogether.

"Good coffee, huh?" Brent said.

"The first cup in the morning is always the best," I told him. Ashley nodded her head.

"Doughnut?" Brent asked, offering me the bag.

"Thanks."

"Definitely," Ashley agreed.

I reached into the bag and picked out a double chocolate. Doughnuts and coffee—our version of the elegant breakfast buffet, even if we were sitting on the curb outside our squat.

I stretched, trying to work some of the kinks out of my back. When I woke up in the morning I was usually so stiff that I felt like an old woman. Sleeping on the ground, or a desk, or a concrete floor didn't ever make for a good night's sleep. Being on the streets meant always being sore, or hungry, or tired, and sometimes all three at once.

"So what's up for today?" Ashley asked.

"I figured we hang, see **some** people, kick around . . . you know, the usual," Brent answered.

"But what about making some money?" I asked.

"Taken care of," he said.

"It is?" Ashley asked.

"What did you think I was doing when I was on my own yesterday?" Brent asked.

"I can think of a lot of things you could have been doing," Ashley replied.

It wasn't unusual for Brent to go off by himself. Sometimes he'd be gone for twenty minutes, sometimes hours and hours. He'd get in a mood, like he was restless, irritated—or maybe like he had something better to do, someplace more important to be. If he hadn't felt so responsible for me and Ashley, he probably would have been gone more often. One thing we could count on: he never left us overnight.

"What I was doing was taking care of us. I got everything we need for today. Everything except water."

"Water?" I asked.

He nodded. "You can't squeegee without—"

"Wait! No way! I'm not doing it!" Ashley snapped.

"Doing what?" I asked.

"I won't be a squeegee kid," Ashley said. "You've seen kids standing on the streets cleaning windshields, haven't you?"

"Yeah, of course," I said.

"And did it look like a lot of fun to you?" she asked.

"It isn't supposed to be fun. It's a good way to earn money," Brent said, patiently. "Besides, I've already got the pail and the squeegees."

Brent took the pack off his back, set it down, and opened it up. He produced three squeegees—the metal-and-rubber things you use at a gas station to clean off your windshield.

"You bought those yesterday?" I asked.

"Bought?" Brent asked, sounding shocked. "You are such a kidder! Nobody said anything about *buying*. I said I *got* them yesterday."

"I don't care whether you *made* them with your own hands," Ashley said. "I don't want to do it."

"We have to do something if we want to eat today," Brent replied.

"Then let's just panhandle."

"But we can get more money by doing this," Brent said, holding up one of the squeegees.

"And we can get more hassles that way, as well," Ashley said, emphatically.

"Sure, there could be some hassles, but—"

"It's nothing *but* hassles!" Ashley shouted, cutting him off.

"And because you don't want to do it, then we just don't do it, is that what you're saying?" Brent demanded. "Does that seem fair?"

"Is it fair that we do it just because *you* want to?" she demanded.

"How about if we vote?" he proposed.

"Fine with me."

They both turned to me. I hated it when they did this. No matter which way I went it was guaranteed that somebody would be mad at me. You should never put somebody in the middle like that. It made me think of the last days before my parents finally separated. When it happened, I was almost grateful—at least nobody was yelling at anybody any more. Little did I know what would happen after that. It would make me wish my parents had never split up.

"Well?" Ashley asked me. "What do you want to do?"

"Um . . . I don't really know."

"Don't be a wimp," Brent said. "Yes or no?"

"Yeah, make a decision."

"How can I make a decision when I don't even really understand what you two are arguing about?"

"Come on, Dana, you can't tell me that you never saw kids cleaning windshields at street corners."

"I've seen it," I admitted.

It was hard to miss if you hung around downtown at all. I even remembered the first time I saw it happen. I couldn't have been more than seven or eight. I was with my mother and we were heading downtown to meet my father for lunch. I was in the back seat—my sister was in her car seat beside me—and we stopped for a red light. These kids came running toward the car. My mother hit the door-lock button and told me not to be scared. I hadn't even thought about being scared until she told me not to—then I was. These kids surrounded the car and started cleaning all the windows. One of the kids—a girl—smiled and waved at me through the window, but I was too afraid to wave back. Then, just before the light changed, my mother opened the window just a crack and handed them a dollar and we drove away.

"So what is it you don't understand?" Brent asked. "You walk out into the street when the cars stop and ask if they want their windshields washed. If they don't, you don't. If they do, you do. There's nothing more to it."

"Nothing more except for getting run over!"

"Come on, Ash, nobody's going to run you down!" Brent argued.

"I've heard of people getting brushed by cars as they speed away. And how about that guy . . . what was his name? . . . Kevin, I think . . . who got brained by the side mirror of that truck?"

"His brain was scrambled before he got hit by the mirror," Brent said. "In fact, that's probably *why* he got hit. It won't happen if you're careful."

"Well, what about the cops, then?" she said. "It's illegal to squeegee."

"It's not illegal to squeegee. It's illegal to be on the road," Brent corrected her.

"Well. Unless people start driving on the sidewalk, that's the only place where you *can* squeegee," Ashley said.

"It's just a ticket if they catch you, and most of the time they don't even want to catch you," Brent said. "They just chase you away, that's all."

"Has either of you ever gotten a ticket?" I asked.

They both shook their heads.

"Has either of you ever been hit or brushed by a car?"

"Not me," Brent said.

"I was almost hit once," Ashley said.

"Almost doesn't count. So, are we going to do it?" Brent asked.

"You said the money was better, right?" I was thinking about another night in a motel room, and we needed money for that.

"It can be very good," Brent said.

"Ashley, can we earn more doing this than panhandling?" She reluctantly nodded her head.

"Then let's try it for a bit. Okay?"

Ashley didn't answer right away. Then she muttered, "I don't like it, but I'll do it."

"All right! So let's get to it," Brent said. "First, we have to find a good corner."

"How about this one?" I asked.

"I was thinking of going down closer to the lake."

"What's wrong with here?" I was pretty sure I'd actually seen squeegee kids on this street before.

"Yeah, let's just stay here," Ashley said. "It's bad enough having to do this without having to go on a major hike first."

Brent looked around hesitantly. "I guess this would be okay."

He got up and walked around to the back of the building we'd slept in, and when he came back he was carrying a pail. He must have stashed it somewhere out there the night before. He offered it to me. "Get this filled with water."

"Water? Where do I get water from?" I asked.

"One of these stores. Just go in and ask," Brent said.

"Why me?"

"Think about it," Brent said. "Who are they more likely to help, me or you?"

"He's got a point there," Ashley agreed.

"Maybe you should come with me, then," I said to Ashley. She shrugged. "Why not?"

"Try the doughnut shop first," Brent suggested, handing me the bucket and dropping the three squeegees into it.

Ashley and I made our way over to the doughnut shop and walked in. There was a lineup at the counter and most of the tables were occupied.

"Let's just go to the washroom and fill up the—"

"Get out of here!" A man—balding and wearing a dirty white apron—came stomping toward us. He looked angry, his eyes blazing, a scowl on his face. I started for the door to leave.

"We just wanted to use the washroom," Ashley said, standing her ground.

"Washrooms only for customers!" he screamed.

"We *are* customers," Ashley said, holding up her coffee cup with the store's name emblazoned across it.

"You not customers! You *filthy* squeegee kids! Get out of my store!"

"Come on, we just want to—"

"Out! Out! Out!" he screamed, lurching toward us in a threatening manner. I backed away farther, but Ashley wouldn't budge.

"Stavros! You stop!" A woman charged across the shop and parked herself right between the man and Ashley. The two of them, hands flying in the air, began yelling at each other in a language I didn't understand. This was our chance to get away. I grabbed Ashley by the arm and tugged. She shook her head and stayed put.

Finally the man scowled and walked away. The woman turned around to face us.

"Ignore husband. You girls need water to do squeegee?" she asked.

"Yeah . . . yes, please," I said.

"Come, come," she said.

She led us away from the washrooms and behind the counter, and we followed. The man eyed us walking by and muttered something under his breath. I was grateful I couldn't understand what he was saying. The woman led us through a set of swinging doors into the back room.

"Give bucket," she said, taking it from Ashley.

She put it into one of a set of big double sinks and turned on the hot water, then grabbed a bottle of dishwashing liquid and squirted it in. "Make better clean," she said. "How old you girls?"

"We're sixteen," Ashley told her.

"No look sixteen. 'Specially her," she said, pointing at me.

"We are, though," Ashley replied.

"You like to do squeegee on cars?" she asked.

"Not really, but we have to earn a living," Ashley said.

"Get job to earn living."

"It's not that easy to get a job," I said.

"You can have job here. Clean up back, wash cups, help make doughnuts."

"But what about your husband?" Ashley asked. "He doesn't even want us in the store."

"Half store *my* store. You work in *my* half!"

"You'd give us a job?" I asked, amazed.

She shrugged. "Why not? Get clean clothes you could work. Pay not great—minimum—and place gets hot, but we treat people good."

"Your husband would treat us good?" Ashley asked.

"He has big mouth, but bigger heart."

The water was overflowing the bucket and she reached over and turned off the tap. She picked up the bucket and pulled it out of the sink, water sloshing over the sides, and handed it to Ashley. She strained under the weight.

"Thanks for the water," I said.

"You girls maybe want job?" she asked.

"Let us think about it," Ashley replied.

"Good. Think. Better to have job inside than on streets," she said.

"We'd better get going." Ashley started to walk away, but I hesitated.

"Thanks for the water . . . and for the job offer . . . I really appreciate it," I said, and then I hurried to catch up with Ashley.

"Come back if want more water . . . any time . . . come back!" she called out.

I ran, caught up to Ashley, and held the door open for her.

"That was a good offer," I said.

"What, to work at the doughnut place?"

"Yeah, we could earn money and—"

"You can't earn anything. You're underage and on the run, and I bet you don't even have a social insurance number, do you?"

I shook my head. "But you could work there."

She laughed. "If I wanted a crappy job earning minimum wage there's a hundred places I'd rather work than some stinking doughnut shop with Stavros hanging around. Let's just stick with this."

EVERY TIME THE LIGHT changed to red we walked between the rows of cars, waving our squeegees and asking if anyone wanted their windshield washed. Some people rolled down their windows and offered us money. Others waved their arms in the air and yelled and told us not to touch their cars, or they called us names. Most people didn't react at all. Or I guess they reacted by trying not to react. They pretended we weren't even there. They stared straight ahead at some picture in the distance—some picture that didn't include us.

It was strange. Them on the inside of their cars. Us on the outside. We were separated by only a thin piece of glass but it was like we were in different worlds: inside and outside. I'd never felt so much *outside* in my life. I couldn't help thinking about the time long ago when I'd been inside the car—me, my sister, and my mom. It was strange. It was less like a memory and more like some movie I'd once watched and half forgotten. I couldn't help wondering what would happen if my mother drove up right now and stopped here at the lights. Would she recognize me? Or would she even notice me as she stared straight ahead?

When I'd first left home I thought about my mother coming and looking for me. She had to know I was in the city . . . where else would I go? Besides, there was the with-drawal from my bank account. They could have traced that, and she would have known for sure where I'd started, even if I wasn't there any more. If she'd really been looking she would have found me. The city was big, but not *that* big.

In the beginning I felt startled every time I saw a car that looked like ours. It was amazing how many SUVs were the same make and colour as my mother's. But with each passing day and each mistaken vehicle I reacted less, until now I hardly noticed.

Part of me also wondered if she even wanted to look for me. It was probably easier without me around. No calls from the school, no fighting about things, no more arguments with my stepfather about me or with me.

Did she ever wonder why things had turned around and why I started getting into so much trouble? I'd heard her talking to my teacher on the phone. She blamed it all on my father . . . him getting involved with "that woman"—that's what my mother called her, *that woman*—and then my father being transferred out to the West Coast. It was easy to blame it all on him. And he did deserve some blame, but not for this—

A car horn blared and I jumped back to reality.

Brent was screaming at me, "Get off the road, Dana!"

The light had changed and the traffic was starting up again. I stood between the two rows of traffic and waited until the last car moved off before I ran over to the safety of the sidewalk.

"Be more careful," Ashley warned me. "You don't want to get hit."

"Don't worry about that," Brent said. "Nobody wants to mess up their shiny car by hitting you."

"That's reassuring."

"At least we're making some good cash," Ashley said.

"Yeah," Brent agreed. "So far we've made almost forty bucks."

"That's great," I said. "Do you want me to go and get some clean water?"

"Don't bother," he said.

"But this water is getting pretty dirty."

"Who cares?" he asked.

"The people in the cars?"

"They don't even expect the water to be clean."

"Then what do they expect?" I asked.

"They expect us not to damage their precious cars, and they're grateful when we don't," he said. "That's the real reason they give us money."

"That, and because they feel sorry for us," Ashley added.

"Enough talk. The lights are getting ready to change again so let's get ready to—"

"Hey, what the hell do you think you're doing?" screamed out an angry voice.

I spun around. There were five kids, three boys and two girls, dressed all punky, marching toward us. Two of them had buckets and all of them were holding squeegees.

"This is our corner!" screamed one of the boys as they advanced on us.

I took a step backwards, retreating slightly behind Brent. They outnumbered us, but Brent was bigger then any of them.

"You better move on!" one of the boys screamed. "Or else!"

"Or else what?" Brent demanded.

"Or else this." The boy—he seemed like their leader—lifted up his shirt to expose a knife sticking out of the top of his pants! A second kid did the same thing.

I took another step back, still clutching the squeegee but holding it farther in front of me for protection—a squeegee against a knife . . . not a great choice.

"I'm *real* scared," Brent snapped sarcastically. Suddenly, out of nowhere, he had a knife in *his* hand! I turned to Ashley . . . *she* was holding a knife *too*!

"You really want to do this?" Brent demanded loudly. "Right out here on the street?"

"You move or we're gonna dance, right here!" growled the leader of the group.

Brent stood there, silent, unmoving, glaring at them glaring at him. Nobody was moving. What was going to—?

"You want it, it's yours," Brent said, and I felt a rush of relief. "We've already collected enough money for today."

I backed away and Ashley followed. Brent stood his ground for a while longer and then began backing off too. He moved away slowly, still holding the knife in front of him, standing between them and us. Finally, feeling that he was at a safe distance, Brent spun around and came after us.

The gang yelled out insults. Brent turned back around and gave them the finger.

"Let them have the corner," Brent said, "for all the good it's going to do them. Cops will be here soon."

"They will?" I asked.

"Sure. We've been working the corner for almost two hours. Somebody's probably complained already."

"I'm just glad we got away," I said. "I didn't know you guys carried knives!"

"You have to protect yourself somehow," Brent said. "I'll get you one."

"I don't want a knife!" I protested.

"Doesn't matter if you want one or not," Ashley said. "This isn't the suburbs any more, remember? Do you think I *like* carrying a knife around?"

Brent got a confused look on his face. "I thought you *did* like having a knife."

" 'Like' isn't the right word. I just know I need one. And so do you," Ashley said, tapping me on the shoulder.

"It just wouldn't feel right."

"Would it feel better to have somebody attack you and have no way of defending yourself?" Ashley asked.

"Of course not."

"You know, I can't always be around to take care of you," Brent said. "And besides, sometimes I might need you to back me up, the way Ashley just did."

"Me, back *you* up?" I asked in astonishment. "Even if I had a knife I wouldn't know what to do with it."

"It's not like I'm an expert," Ashley said.

"I couldn't stab anybody."

"Nobody's asking you to do that," Brent said.

"Besides, you really don't know," Ashley added.

"Know what?"

"Whether or not you could stab somebody. *You never know*," she said, her voice going all quiet.

My instant reaction was to tell her I could never do that . . . and then I thought about it, and realized that wasn't entirely true.

chapter eight

"YOU'RE EVEN BETTER with a brush than you are with a spray can."

I didn't bother turning around. A bunch of strangers had been complimenting me on the painting I was working on, but this voice I knew. It was Robert, the guy who had given me the card that led me to Sketches.

"It's okay," I mumbled.

"Nicki told me you'd dropped in a few days ago. I'm glad to see you've come back again. So, what do you call it?"

"The painting?"

He nodded.

"I haven't really thought about it," I said.

"Every painting needs a name," he said. "The bigger of the two girls is you, right?"

"Yes . . . it *is* me." I was kind of amazed that he'd figured that out. I didn't think it even looked that much like me.

"The eyes. I could tell by the eyes," he explained.

"But they're not even finished."

"Still. I can see your eyes in those eyes," he said. "And the second girl, the smaller one, is that your sister?"

My mouth dropped open in shock.

"Am I right?" he asked.

I nodded my head dumbly. "But . . . but how did you know?"

"Just a guess."

"You should be working one of those psychic hotline phone things," I said.

He laughed. "I had a few clues. The two figures have similarly shaped faces and the hair colour is almost identical, and they both have the same unfinished eyes. They look like sisters. You're very good."

I smiled. I loved doing art. I also loved people complimenting me on my work. Getting compliments on anything hadn't happened much over the last couple of years.

"People usually paint the things or people that they miss the most," he added.

I didn't know what to say. It bugged me that he was already that far into my head, but he was right . . . I did miss my sister tremendously. There were only three years between us, but I felt a lot older. Since Dad had left I'd felt more like I was the second adult, the second parent, to her. Candice. She was such a sweet kid. She liked everybody and everybody liked her. That was the hardest part about leaving the way I did. I just hoped she didn't think it had anything to do with her. The last thing she needed was to feel like somebody else had abandoned her.

"And I bet she misses you a lot, too," he said.

I felt like I'd been kicked in the stomach, and tears began to well up in my eyes. I bit down on the inside of my cheek to try and keep them from coming out. Crying didn't solve anything.

"How long has it been since you last saw her?"

"Over a month," I answered, my voice barely a whisper. I thought about my sister all the time . . . what she was doing, what she was thinking. It was like I hadn't even realized it till he said that. I wished I could have said goodbye to her, explained why I had to leave . . .

"Does she know you're okay? Have you called home?"

I shook my head.

"Do you think you can?" he said.

"Maybe you should mind your own business!" I snapped. I was surprised by my own anger. I could see he was surprised, too. The burst of anger dried up the tears in my eyes.

"I'm really sorry that I upset you. I didn't mean to do that," he apologized.

"I guess I shouldn't have yelled," I mumbled.

"That's okay too. Sometimes things hurt and it's only natural to react. I'll try not to poke you there again." His expression looked sad and sorry, and I suddenly felt bad for yelling at him. He hadn't meant anything wrong.

"Tell you what," he said, "how about if I go and get us a couple of coffees and then I'll go and find you another brush."

"Why do I need another brush?" I asked.

"You need one with finer bristles to finish the eyes. You do want to finish the eyes, don't you?" he asked.

"I do," I said. "But . . . I just don't quite know how to do it right."

"I can show you," he said. "If you want. Would you like that?"

I nodded.

"Good. Let me go and get us those coffees and then I'll give you a little art lesson."

He started to walk toward the kitchen.

"Robert?"

He stopped and turned around.

"*The Sisters*," I said. "I'm going to call it *The Sisters*."

BETWEEN TALKING TO ROBERT, having him show me how to do the fine work around the eyes, and then getting cleaned up, it was almost night by the time I got out of Sketches. I was late. I trotted along the street hoping that they'd still be there. What if they weren't? Where would I go? How would I find them? Who would take care of me, and . . . ?

Brent was sitting on the edge of a fountain and Ashley was standing off to the side. She was panhandling, but it didn't look as though she was doing too well.

"Sorry I'm late," I said as I settled in beside him.

"Now that you're here, we'd better get moving," Brent said. He stood up right away and started walking. I was getting the feeling that he was in another of his dark moods.

"Where are we going?" I asked as Ashley and I trailed after him.

"You'll see."

"We didn't think you were coming," Ashley said.

"Not coming? Where else would I go?"

"I don't know, maybe you were planning on hanging out at that art centre place all night?" Brent said.

"Yeah, well, it would be cool to spend more time there."

"There's nothing there that's going to make us money or give us a place to sleep tonight," Brent snapped back.

"It's more than that!" I argued.

"Actually, it's less than that," he said. "While you're fooling around in there, we're out here trying to get together enough cash to—"

"Give it a rest," Ashley said, cutting him off.

"You could come along with me and see for yourself," I suggested.

"Me?" Brent questioned incredulously. "I'm way too old to be doing any finger-painting."

"It's not Kindergarten stuff! I did a really good painting today!" I protested.

"Well *I'd* like to see it," Ashley said. "Maybe I'll come with you the next time you go."

"Great." Brent scowled. "Then I'll have to do the work of *three* people. Are you two planning on eating?"

"Actually, they have food at Sketches," I said.

"They do?" Brent had been walking quickly, leading us down an alley, but now he stopped walking, turned around, and suddenly seemed interested. "Why didn't you tell me that before?"

"I did . . . sort of. Remember those muffins I brought you the other day?" After the first time, when I hadn't shared the food I'd gotten, I'd made a point of letting them have all the food I pocketed at Sketches.

"Is that where they came from?" he asked.

"Where did you think I got them?"

"I didn't think," he said. "I figured you just ripped them off or something."

"Yeah, that really sounds like Dana," Ashley said sarcastically.

"So, if we go to this Sketches place they'll feed us?" Brent asked.

"Not feed you, but they usually have some food. At least muffins and bagels and juice and milk."

"Those weren't even good muffins," he grumbled.

"They weren't bad," Ashley said.

"So I'm walking all the way there for a day-old muffin?"

"And juice and milk," I added, a bit weakly.

"Oh, great, that makes it better, milk and muffins. I'll pass." He started walking again.

"Come on, Brent, would it kill you to drop in one afternoon and have a look?" Ashley demanded.

"It wouldn't kill me, but it ain't gonna help me either. I'll just—"

Suddenly two guys jumped out from behind a dumpster and smashed into Brent, sending him tumbling into the wall! Before he could react or even fall over they grabbed him by both arms and pinned him against the bricks!

Ashley rushed to his defence. "Hey, what do you think you're—?"

A third guy jumped out of a doorway on the other side of the alley and pushed her from behind and she toppled forward, hitting the wall and then crumpling to the pavement! Before I could even think to react I was grabbed by both arms—a guy was holding me on one side and a girl on the other. They were both about my age . . . they were all about our age.

"Don't even think about fighting!" the girl yelled.

I wasn't thinking about anything—I just felt fear, terror— all I wanted to do was run, but there was no point in even trying. The two sets of powerful hands held me between them, and I was powerless to resist.

Ashley started to struggle to her feet, and the guy who'd knocked her down stepped forward again and kicked her in the ribs! She groaned and then gasped as the air rushed out of her lungs and she collapsed back to the ground.

"Leave her alone!" Brent screamed.

Now the guy who'd kicked Ashley rushed over and punched Brent in the face as he stood there, pinned against the wall! Brent's nose exploded and blood started pouring down his face.

"Brent!" I yelled.

The guy spun around to face me, and his look of rage made my blood freeze.

"Do you want some of this?" he yelled, waving his fist in my face.

I shook my head slightly, unable to speak.

"Not a sound from you," he snarled.

I started to sob, tears just flying out of my eyes.

"No crying!" he shouted. "You cry and I'll give you something to cry about!"

He stepped forward and I closed my eyes and turned my head away, waiting for the punch to come. Instead I felt his hands grab my face, and my eyes popped open. He moved in close, pushing his face right into mine so close that I was overwhelmed by his stale, awful breath. I bit down on the inside of my cheek to try to stifle my tears.

"That's better," he said. A smile—an awful, evil smile—came to his lips. "You ain't half bad-looking. A little dirty maybe, but not bad." He released his grip on my face . . . thank goodness. But then he reached down and grabbed my breasts! I struggled to get away but I was held in place on both sides and he pressed against me.

"Leave her alone!" Brent screamed.

The guy spun around, but released me. "You need more medicine?"

"You can have our money," Brent said, blood pouring down his face, his shirt all wet and stained.

"We can have your money and anything else we want!"

"Take our money and go before the police come. You don't think that anybody's noticed what's happening? Look!"

I turned toward where Brent was motioning with his chin. There were people on the street. A steady stream of them passed by the opening to the alley. As I looked, a man slowed and peered into the shadows.

"Just take the money," Brent said. "Let me go and I'll give it to you."

"Nobody's letting anybody go. Where is it?" he demanded.

"In my pocket. Right front pants pocket."

He stuck his hand into Brent's pocket and pulled it inside out, coins popping out into the air and showering down on the pavement. He opened his hand to reveal more coins and some bills and a plastic bag . . . a plastic bag holding marijuana! When had he bought that?

"Looky what we got here," he said, holding the bag up. "Some money and a little bonus."

"Just take it and go," Brent said.

"Is this all you got?" he demanded.

"That's all we got . . . I swear," Brent said.

"And the girls? Do they have any money?"

"None," Brent said. "I don't let them have money. I keep it all so that it'll be safe."

The guy laughed. His laugh was as evil as his smile. "Yeah, you kept it *real* safe," he snarled. He turned around, and I was terrified he was going to come back toward me. "Now if either of you girls decide you want to be *really* safe you can stop hanging out with this loser and come with me. Let her go," he ordered, and the two released my arms. "Who knows, maybe I could even figure out a way for you two ladies to make some serious coin, if you know what I mean." That sick smile returned to his face. I noticed he was missing a front tooth and the remaining teeth were yellow and stained.

"You got the money. Now leave us alone," Brent said.

Just then someone stopped at the entrance to the alley. It looked as though he was taking a long, hard look, maybe thinking about coming to see what the noise was all about.

"Yeah, you're right," the guy said. "Let him go, too."

The two other guys released Brent and he slumped forward. The first guy started to walk away down the alley, away from the street. I felt a sense of relief, and—

He turned back suddenly and kicked Brent in the side of the head, and Brent bounced against the wall and then crumpled to the ground!

"Don't you go telling me what to do or when to leave, you understand!" he bellowed. "And you better remember that, faggot, for the next time we meet!"

He took off again, and the other four trailed behind him, laughing and joking as they walked. I stood motionless, watching them go, terrified they might turn back around. Suddenly my feet became unstuck from the pavement and I had to fight the urge to just run away. I couldn't do that. Instead I rushed over to Ashley and helped her as she staggered to her feet. She cringed in pain and clutched her side.

"Ashley, are you all right?" I gasped.

"I'm . . . I'm okay . . . Brent?" she called out.

He started to struggle to his feet and then tumbled back over. We rushed over. He took my hand and used it to pull himself up. Blood still poured from his nose, and now the whole side of his face was scraped and cut and raw.

"You're hurt bad!"

"Not as bad as I'm going to hurt him," he snarled. Brent reached down and pulled his knife out of his sock.

"What are you doing?" I demanded.

"I'm going to get our money back." He started to walk in the direction they'd gone, stumbling over his feet and practically tumbling over again. I caught up to him and grabbed him on one side. Ashley grabbed his other arm.

"All you're going to do is let him finish killing you," Ashley said. "You're too hurt to go after him, and I'm too hurt to help you."

"We can't just let him do that to us!" Brent snapped.

"We won't," Ashley said. "We won't let him get away with anything. We just need to let it go for now."

Brent stopped straining against us and I could feel him relax. Ashley let go of his arm and I did the same.

"You know when he said to remember him?" Brent asked, his voice barely a whisper.

Both Ashley and I nodded. I didn't think I'd ever forget him.

"I'll remember him," Brent said. "And maybe not today, or tomorrow, but sooner or later it'll happen."

"That's right," Ashley said. "Now let's just go and get cleaned up and find someplace to stay tonight."

"Shouldn't we go to the hospital?" I asked.

"Why?" Brent asked.

"Your nose, and Ashley's ribs . . . you two are hurt!" I exclaimed.

"I just need to lie down," Ashley said.

"Me too. Let me get cleaned up first and then just lie down . . . I feel a little bit dizzy." Brent staggered a bit and Ashley and I both grabbed him again to steady him on his feet.

"I know a place where we can crash for the night," Brent said. "It's not far from here. We'll just cut down the alley and—"

"You want us to go down the alley?" I said.

"It's shorter that way."

"But *they* went down the alley."

"They're long gone," Brent pointed out. "Probably using our money to buy some chemicals."

"I just don't think we should go that way," I protested.

"It'll be okay," Brent said. "Come on."

He started walking, with Ashley still supporting him. I hesitated for a few seconds and then started after them. I didn't want to go, but I couldn't stay there by myself. Cautiously we moved. I strained to look up ahead, trying to see behind every dumpster and trash can, and into the depressions of the doors and the shadows cast by the buildings. I couldn't see anybody, but then again I didn't see those kids either.

We reached the end of the alley and Brent directed us through a hole in a fence where three boards were missing. He went through first, followed by Ashley and then me. We were standing in a parking lot. The pavement was all buckled and there were weeds growing in the cracks. There was a shed sitting behind a building and trash bags and furniture all around it. As we closed in I realized it was a clothing drop box and there was a big sign on the building: "Salvation Army." We stopped beside the drop box.

"Here we are," Brent said. "This is where we're going to sleep tonight."

"We're going to sleep in the Salvation Army shelter?" I asked. We'd never done that before. Shelters asked for ID and I didn't have any and—

"Not in the Salvation Army shelter," he said. "In the shelter of the Salvation Army clothing drop box."

"We're going to what?"

"We're going to sleep in the box." He pointed at the gigantic wood-and-metal box where people dropped off clothes and things for the Salvation Army to sell.

He reached over and pulled open the big drawer-like slot. It was a large opening—big enough to take a green garbage bag filled with clothes. I'd gone with my mother before to put some of our old clothes in a box just like this one where we live . . . where *they* live.

"Give me a boost," Ashley said.

Brent bent down and cupped his hands together, and Ashley put her foot into his hands, using them as a step. She climbed up into the slot and disappeared from sight. Her head reappeared a couple of seconds later.

"There's enough space for all of us," she said.

"Is there anything for us to sleep on in there?" Brent asked.

"Lots of bags filled with clothes. It'll be a soft night's sleep."

"Great," Brent said. He turned to me. "Let me give you a boost."

"Into there?" I moved back a half a step.

"You got a better idea? It's warm and it's dry."

"But what if somebody comes? What if they drop something into the box on top of us?"

"The place is closed for the night and the gate is locked up. The only way in here is the way we came, and I can't picture anybody coming in through the fence with a donation," Brent said.

"But still . . . it's a *clothing drop box*," I said, emphasizing each word. "We can't sleep in there."

"I'm telling you we *can*. I've done it dozens of times." Brent paused. "Look, Dana, my head is hurting really bad. I need to lie down. You coming or not?"

Reluctantly I came forward and Brent bent down again, cupping his hands together. I stepped up and Ashley offered me a hand and I slid, head first, into the box. The slot slammed closed behind me and I was engulfed in darkness. I felt a surge of panic. Then there was light as the slot opened back up. I looked up and saw Brent's silhouette against the light. He climbed in, and now the slot stayed open.

"I wedged a board in to keep it open," Brent said.

"Thanks," I mumbled.

"Once we've got everything sorted out in here we'll close it up so we can sleep."

"Are you sure we won't get in trouble for sleeping in here?" I asked, apprehensively.

"We won't get in trouble . . . if nobody finds us," Brent said. He began to chuckle, and it felt so good to hear. "We'll be long gone before they open up in the morning."

"Besides," Ashley said, "even if they did catch us they wouldn't do anything."

"They wouldn't?"

"Nah," Brent said, shaking his head. "This is the Salvation Army. The worst they'd do is force us to eat breakfast, read to us from the Bible, and try to convince us to stay in their shelter tonight."

"Sleeping in a shelter wouldn't be so bad," I said.

"You ever sleep in a shelter?" Brent asked.

"No," I admitted. "You know that."

"Believe me, this is better."

"Are you serious?"

"Well, better than most of them. It's not that they don't try to help," Brent said.

"Then what's wrong with them?"

"They have lots of rules and they ask lots of questions," Ashley said.

"What sort of questions?"

"Like, 'Are you carrying any weapons?' or 'How old are you?'" Ashley answered.

That would be a problem for me. Things would be easier once I was sixteen—if I *lived* to be sixteen.

"How about if we stop talking and go to sleep," Brent said.

"Are you sure you should do that?" I asked. "After a head injury you're supposed to be woken up every couple of hours," I explained.

"You are?"

"Yeah. I remember that from my first aid course at school. Do you want me to wake you up?"

"Yeah. In the morning. Let's get to sleep." He reached up and adjusted the board holding the slot. It closed almost all the way, with only a sliver of light still coming in. Brent lay down on the far side of the box.

I settled into the bags, my head close to the little shaft of light. I needed to sleep too, but maybe I needed to stay up for a while even more. I'd listen for sounds coming from outside, and even more important, listen for the sounds of Brent sleeping.

chapter nine

"DANA, YOU'RE JUST IN TIME!" Nicki exclaimed as I walked through the front door.

"In time for what?" I asked anxiously.

"In time to go."

"Go . . . but I just got here! Are you closed for the day?"

"Open for business, but we're just leaving, and you can come with us."

"Come with you where?" I asked.

"That would be telling. Come on, trust me," she said with a smile. "We will be doing some genuine, true, 100 percent *street* art."

"What sort of street art?"

Nicki laughed. "Did you come here to play Twenty Questions or do some art?"

"Art."

"Then shut up and come with us."

I joined in with the little group—Nicki, Robert, another counsellor, and five kids. Three of them I knew, and the other two I'd seen around before but had never talked to. Two of the guys were carrying large canvas bags.

"That's a nice top," one of the girls said to me.

"Yeah, really nice," one of the boys agreed.

"Thanks," I mumbled.

"Is it new?" Nicki asked.

"Yeah. I picked it up this morning." That was true. I had picked it up out of one of the bags that were in the drop box with us. We'd been looking for something to replace Brent's blood-stained and ruined shirt, but we'd also found a couple of things that Ashley and I liked. I felt a little bad taking something meant for the Salvation Army, but Brent just laughed and said that they'd be giving them to poor people anyway, and there was hardly anybody who was poorer than us.

Brent had insisted that we put everything we didn't take neatly back into the bags. He made sure that we didn't damage anything or make a mess, because he said we should "respect" the Salvation Army people. He kept talking about how they were doing "God's work," and he even quoted from the Bible a few times. It was strange. I'd never heard him talk like that before. He sounded like he was some sort of minister or something. It was obvious that he'd spent more than one Sunday in a church somewhere. I wanted to ask, but I figured that was against the rules. People talked if they wanted to talk.

Brent had looked terrible that morning. His face was bloody and swollen and he was complaining about a bad headache. Ashley wasn't much better. She had lifted up her top to show me the bruises over her ribs, and she winced in pain whenever she tried to take a deep breath. I had wanted to stay with them, but they had told me they were just going to "lie low" all day and that this was a good day for me to "goof off" at the drop-in centre. Besides, I thought maybe I could pick up some food to bring back, even if it was just day-old muffins and milk.

Before I left I went and got them coffee and doughnuts. Those thugs hadn't taken all of our money. Brent kept most of the money in his sock—thank goodness. I was going to meet them back at the parking lot around five. I guess that meant we were going to spend another night in the box. Funny, compared to some of the places we'd stayed, the clothing drop box was almost luxurious, like our own private little apartment. I'd felt safe and warm in there.

"How about right here?" Nicki asked as we abruptly came to a stop.

Robert looked around. He was studying something, but I couldn't figure out what. "Looks good to me," he agreed.

We were standing in a little park at a busy intersection. Traffic zoomed by on both sides, and people—moving almost as fast—bumped along on the sidewalk. I sat down on one of the two benches.

"You haven't even started to work and you're already taking a break?" Nicki said.

I quickly got to my feet, although my legs felt heavy and tired. Actually *all* of me felt heavy and tired. I had hardly slept at all. I'd been worried about Brent and had tried to stay awake to listen for his breathing. Then when I finally did drift off I was haunted by bad dreams. I could see that guy—that look in his eyes, that evil smile—I could hear his laugh, smell his foul breath. I shuddered. Then morning finally arrived and the sun heated up that little metal box so much that it felt like an oven.

"Take this," Nicki said as she handed me a little whisk broom.

"What do you want me to do with this?"

"Dana, my dear, it's a broom. What do you *think* I want you to do with it?"

"I just don't know what you want me to sweep . . . *why* you want me to sweep."

"You have to sweep to properly prepare our canvas," she explained.

"Our canvas? I don't see any canvas . . . is it in one of those bags?"

Nicki laughed. "No. You're standing on it."

I looked down anxiously. There was nothing beneath my feet except cement.

"The sidewalk is our canvas," Nicki said.

"We're going to *paint* the sidewalk?" I was having trouble with the concept.

"Not paint. Chalk."

I went from confused to even more confused.

"You sweep and I'll explain," Nicki said. "This whole big block of concrete you're standing on is going to be our canvas, and chalk is going to be our medium," Nicki explained. "You ever use chalk to draw on the sidewalk?"

"When I was a kid."

"As opposed to the old woman that you are now?" Robert piped up.

"You know what I mean. When I was a *little* kid. I'd use it for hopscotch or writing my name on the driveway."

"Same idea, but a little more complicated. Show her the book."

The other counsellor—I didn't know her name—rummaged around in one of the canvas bags and produced a big, thick, glossy-looking book. She handed the book to Nicki, who showed it to me.

"It's an art book," I said.

"It's an art book filled with the most famous paintings in history. And we're going to reproduce one of those pictures right here on the pavement."

"We are? How?"

Nicki's brow furrowed. "I thought you could show us how to do it since you've had all that experience using chalk to play hopscotch."

"Me?" I exclaimed. "I don't know how to . . ."

I let the sentence trail off as Nicki and Robert and the other counsellor broke into broad smiles.

"Don't worry, it's not hard," Nicki said.

"And we'll walk you guys through it, real slow, step by step. By the end of today you'll be able to do it yourself if you want," Robert said.

"That's right. You get back to sweeping and we'll get everything set up."

IT WAS AMAZING to watch. Right after I finished sweeping Nicki went over the entire square to make sure there wasn't a grain of sand or a speck of dust. She used a large ruler and a measuring tape to make a "frame" on the pavement. The frame was bigger—a lot bigger—than the picture in the book, but in perfect proportion. Then important spots on the painting were measured from the side and marked on the pavement at the same distance from the frame that had already been created.

From there a light outline of faint white chalk was used to start sketching the features of the painting. The other counsellor—I found out her name was Becca—did most of the outlining. Sometimes it looked good the first time. Other times it was wrong and she rubbed it off and retraced it. After watching the process a couple of times Becca asked me to give it a try. It wasn't hard at all. She even said I had a talent for it. I did seem to be able to do it fairly easily.

Becca was nice. She was young—not really that much older than me or the other kids. She was dressed in overalls and sandals. Her hair, the little bit of fuzz that she had, was a shocking shade of pink. And maybe to make up for the lack of hair she had over a dozen earrings, as well as a nose ring and a lip ring.

The next step involved selecting the right shade of chalk to match the colour of the painting. Once that was done it was about as complicated as using crayons and a colouring book to just fill in the outline.

Quickly the painting—at least the chalk reproduction of the painting—came to life. It was a gigantic copy of the picture in the book: *Starry Night*, by Vincent Van Gogh. It was a painting that I'd always loved—the way the lights in the sky seem to actually be alive and move. When it was done, it really did look like the original. And even more amazing than watching the painting come to life was that I was part of creating it.

And it wasn't just me who was amazed. People slowed down as they passed. Some stopped for a few seconds or half a minute. Others stayed for a lot longer. People were really friendly. They watched us work, and the book was propped up for us to work from so they were able to compare our reproduction to the original. They asked questions, or made jokes, or gave us suggestions and compliments. They also gave more than that—they gave money.

Originally I hadn't even noticed the hat sitting beside the painting. That is, I hadn't noticed it until the first coins started dropping in. And of course there weren't just coins. There were bills, including a twenty that was sitting on the top of the pile of change. Every ten or fifteen minutes Nicki or Robert would clean out the money in the hat and slip it into one of the canvas bags. They never removed all of the money, though. Some of the change, and a couple of the bills—including the twenty—were always left behind. Robert said they did that because they wanted people to know that not only were we taking contributions, but we'd be happy to accept *really big* contributions. Both he and Nicki seemed to really know what they were doing.

Speaking of Nicki, where was she? I looked around. I was so occupied by the creation that I hadn't even noticed her leave. She was nowhere to be seen. Then I saw her down the street, walking toward us. She was carrying something. A white plastic bag and some boxes. I watched as she got closer. They looked like pizza boxes! She was carrying pizza! I'd been so immersed in the work that I'd forgotten just how hungry I was.

"Okay, everybody, time to break for lunch," Nicki sang out.

Everybody stopped working as she set the two boxes down on one of the benches. She opened up one of the boxes, and steam and a delicious pizza smell rose up into the air.

"I hope pepperoni is okay," she said. "And I brought along juice and pop and water." She started to unload the drinks from the bag.

I stood up and brushed off my pants. My knees and back felt sore. Being sore was nothing new. Sore and hungry. Cold and wet. Being on the run meant always feeling at least a couple of those all the time. Add in afraid and uncertain and that pretty well covered the whole experience.

"It smells really good." I reached out to take a piece.

"Not so fast," Nicki said. "Look at your hands."

I held them up. They were a filthy combination of dirt and chalk.

"Take one of these," Robert said as he offered me a box of Wet Wipes. "It's the best we can do."

I took two. The white fabric quickly became black. I tossed them in the trash can and grabbed another one as all nine of us tried to get clean. Finally satisfied, I took a piece of pizza.

"Take another one," Nicki said.

I grabbed a second piece and then took a can of Coke. I retreated over to the little postage-stamp-sized piece of grass that the city called a park and sat down. I took a big bite of pizza and washed it down with a slug from the can of Coke. It all tasted very good.

"Mind if I join you?" Nicki asked.

"No, not at all." I shifted slightly to the side to share the spot of grass with her. She settled in beside me.

"No breakfast this morning?" Nicki asked.

"I had a doughnut and a coffee, but I did work up an appetite."

"And my guess is that it wasn't a very good night's sleep, either."

"Not great," I admitted. "How did you know that?"

"Easy. You look like crap!"

"Thanks a lot," I said defensively.

"I'm not trying to insult you, just telling it like it is. How do you *feel*?"

I didn't answer right away. "Like crap."

Nicki laughed. "Well, after a couple of good meals you'll feel better."

"A couple of meals?" I asked.

"Lunch and then dinner," Nicki said.

"Are you buying us supper as well?"

"Nope. We'll be finished long before then. Hopefully you'll be buying *yourself* a good meal."

"If I had any money for supper, don't you think I would have bought myself something more for breakfast?" I asked.

"Breakfast I can't comment on, but I know you'll have money for supper. After paying for the pizza and drinks I still have over ninety dollars left from what we've collected today. So even if nobody's dropped in another dime—and I can tell by looking at the hat that that isn't true—you'll still get around ten bucks."

"I get some of the money?"

"One-ninth of the money. What did you think we were going to do with it?"

"I hadn't really thought about it. I guess I figured it would just go to Sketches, to pay for chalk or your salary."

"Two-ninths of it will go to Sketches because Robert and I are two of the people who helped to create the art."

"But what about Becca?" I asked, pointing at the other counsellor. "Doesn't she work for Sketches too?"

Nicki shook her head. "She's a professional artist who lives in the community."

"But I always see her there, and she's always helping people. She *acts* like she works there."

"And how exactly do people who work at Sketches act?" Nicki questioned.

"I don't know . . . like they know their way around . . . helpful."

"Helpful is good, and she certainly does know her way around Sketches. She's been there longer than I have," Nicki explained. "She's one of our alumni."

"What does that mean?" I asked.

"It means that she started in the program the same way you did. She was a street kid who just dropped in occasionally. But she kept coming, and took some courses from us, and one thing led to another." Nicki shrugged. "Now she has a place to live and makes money from her art."

"She does?"

"Her paintings are quite good. Her work has been exhibited in galleries around the city. I think one of the art critics in the paper described her work as 'fresh, raw, and real.'"

"That sounds pretty good."

"And pretty expensive. Becca told me one of her latest works went for over a thousand dollars."

"But if she's making all that money, why does she come down here to earn a few bucks with chalk?" I asked.

"It has nothing to do with the money. She always gives it to Sketches to buy new supplies. Who do you think bought all this chalk?"

"She did?"

"That and paint and some clay. She's always free to do what she wants with the money she earns today, just as everybody else is. She can afford to give back and she wants to, so she can repay what was given to her. Someday, that might be what you'll do when you make it."

"You think I could be an artist?"

"Could be," she said. "You have a lot of talent. But it could be that you make it in another way."

"What do you mean?" I asked.

"Not everybody is going to be a professional artist. The graduates of Sketches go on to do lots of other things—people have become construction workers, youth workers, bakers. Where do you think we get our endless supply of bagels and buns and muffins? Billy works over at Buns Master, apprenticing to become a baker. He makes sure the owner lets us have all the day-old stuff. And the construction at the centre is being done by another one of our former kids, Brian. People just feel good about paying back the help we've given them, like I know you will someday."

I didn't answer. I didn't know if I'd ever be in a position to help anybody with anything.

"Of course with you, we're still missing the important first step," Nicki said.

"What step is that?"

"We still have to help you."

"You have helped me! You are helping me! You bought me lunch today, and I'm getting money from this, and you let me do some paintings, and I had some bagels and muffins before."

"There's a whole lot more than that we can offer," Nicki said.

I wasn't sure I was ready for anything more.

"We're an art drop-in centre, and that's our primary goal, our mission. But we're also connected to all the other services in the city. I *know* all the services in the city, and more important, the people who run them. If you have a problem, I just might have an answer to where you could go and who you could talk to."

"What sort of problem?" I asked hesitantly.

"Like if you need a place to live, or food, or clothing, or medical treatment, or—"

"Medical treatment?" I asked, cutting her off.

She nodded. "We have connections with doctors and health centres that can offer advice or treatment for sexually transmitted diseases, birth control, drug and alcohol counselling—"

"What about if somebody was hurt?" I paused. "Beaten up."

"You were beaten up?"

"Not me. I'm fine. It's my friends."

"Is that what happened last night that caused you to lose sleep?"

I didn't want to answer, but I nodded my head ever so slightly.

"Do you want to talk about it?" Nicki asked.

"No," I said. "Talking about it won't change anything. I just want to know if there's somebody who could look at them, to see if they're all right. Like a doctor or somebody like that."

"I can arrange it," Nicki said.

"And they won't have to pay, will they? Because we don't have any money."

"No cost and no hassle. They won't even have to give their names if they don't want to. How badly are they hurt?"

"Bren—" I stopped myself. I didn't want to give out his name. It was something I'd learned. Never give out information you didn't need to give out. "My one friend was hit in the head and his face is all scraped up, and my other friend got kicked in the side and her ribs are sore, and she says it hurts to breathe deeply."

"She might have broken or cracked ribs," Nicki said. "It's important to have them looked at. If she doesn't get them properly treated she could get pneumonia. And the hit in the head could have caused a concussion. Did your friend pass out?"

"Not pass out, but he was dizzy and not very steady on his feet."

"Sounds like a concussion. He needs to see somebody. They both need to see somebody. Tell you what, right after lunch I'll go and make a couple of phone calls. I'll find somebody for them to see." She paused. "Who did this to them?"

"I don't know."

"You weren't there, or they didn't tell you, or you don't know the people, or you don't want to tell me about it?" she asked.

"Yes," I said.

She snorted. "Yes to which part?"

"Yes to most of it."

"But you didn't get hurt, right?" Nicki asked. Again she sounded so concerned that I felt bad not telling her, not trusting her with more.

"They didn't hurt me."

"But you were there?" Nicki asked.

"I was there," I said softly.

"And they didn't touch you?"

"I didn't say that," I murmured, my voice barely above a whisper.

Nicki reached over and put a hand on my shoulder. "Are you sure you're okay?"

My whole body shuddered and I had to fight to hold back tears. "They didn't hurt me . . . I'm okay. It's my friends I'm worried about."

"Me too," Nicki said. "If I arrange for them to see somebody, will they go?"

"I'll *make* them go!"

"Sounds like you're a good friend and they're lucky to have you around."

"I'm lucky to have *them* around," I said. "And I'm worried about them." When I left that morning Ashley was clutching her side, and Brent was complaining about how much his head still hurt.

"I'll arrange for the doctor and you arrange for them to go and see her. Okay?"

"Okay."

Nicki smiled. "Now, that wasn't too hard, was it?"

"It wasn't hard at all."

"Sometimes it's difficult to trust people. But we're here to help in any way we can. Now you finish up your lunch, get back to work, and I'll take care of business."

chapter ten

"IT'S NOT MUCH FARTHER," I said.

"Good, because I'm really not enjoying this little stroll, and you still haven't told us where we're going," Brent muttered.

"It's a surprise."

"I've had lots of surprises in my life and not many of them have been good ones," Brent said.

"I hear that," Ashley agreed in a soft voice. "Come on, Dana, where are we going?"

"We're going to see a doctor."

Brent skidded to a stop. "I'm not going to any hospital!" he protested.

"Nobody said anything about a hospital. It's a clinic—a clinic where the doctors take care of people from the street. For free."

"I've heard about places like that," Ashley said.

"I'm not going," Brent insisted.

"You have to go," I pleaded. "You probably have a concussion, and Ashley may have cracked ribs."

"Since when did you become a doctor?" Brent asked sarcastically.

"I'm not a doctor, but I did take a first aid course," I said.

"Was that before or after your hip hop lessons?" Ashley asked sarcastically.

"Same time," I said, answering the question but ignoring the shot. "Besides, that's what Nicki told me."

"Nicki from the drop-in centre?" Ashley asked.

"Yeah."

"Great, just what I need, to get my medical advice from somebody who works in an art drop-in centre!" Brent snapped. "Did she paint you a picture of a doctor?"

"How about you stop being such a jerk and listen to what I have to say!" I answered sharply. "She knows lots of things besides art, and she's smart enough to know that you two need to see a doctor."

"I'm fine!" Brent said.

"Are you?" I asked. I turned to Ashley. "Are you?"

She didn't respond at first, and then she shook her head.

"I know it still must hurt, and you're having trouble breathing, right?"

"It hurts a lot," she admitted. "When I take a deep breath it feels like somebody is sticking a knife into my lungs."

I turned back to Brent. "And you're not going to tell me that your head isn't still hurting at least a little."

"That's where you're wrong," he said. "It isn't hurting a little . . . it feels like it's going to split in two."

"You are such a jerk sometimes," I said. "Quit giving me a hard time and let's have you both looked at. Nobody's going to give you a hassle. Nicki said you don't even have to give them your names if you don't want to."

"And how does she know that?" Brent asked.

"She knows because she arranged it. So how about if you just shut up for a while and let's get the two of you checked out."

"WHICH ONE OF YOU IS DANA?" the woman asked as she walked into the gloomy, dirty, waiting room. It looked more like the sort of place where you'd catch a disease than where you'd be cured of one.

"I am," I said as I put down the newspaper.

"And you have two friends with you, right?"

"Yeah, these two," I said, motioning first to Ashley and then to Brent.

The waiting room was crowded with kids, street kids, and older street people, the sort who slept on heating grates and pushed around shopping carts filled with garbage. There was one woman sitting in the corner having a loud argument with herself—and she seemed to be losing.

"All three of you come this way," the woman said.

The chair I was sitting on groaned as I got to my feet. I was happy to follow her, happy to leave the crowded, foul-smelling room. We entered a little examination room—there was another woman waiting there. She looked young.

"I'm Beth," she said. "Now, which one of you is Dana?"

I held up my hand.

"And you two are . . . ?" she asked.

"We heard we didn't have to give our names," Brent said.

"You don't, but first names are helpful. It stops me from saying, 'Hey you, buddy' all the time," she explained.

"She's Ashley and he's Brent."

"Good to meet you both. So, let me hear about the problem," she began.

"We already told everything to that receptionist, and now we have to tell you, and then we're going to have to explain it all to the doctor again and—"

"You *are* explaining it to the doctor," she said, cutting Brent off.

"You're the doctor?" The amazement in his voice reflected my own shock.

"Yep. Do you want to see my stethoscope?" she asked as she pulled it out of the pocket of her lab coat.

"Yes! I mean, no. I mean, I just didn't think that you were a doctor," he sputtered.

She laughed. "I get that all the time . . . maybe because I look young."

"*Really* young," Ashley added.

"Yeah, really young," she agreed. "I guess when I get older that'll be a good thing, but for now it's a real pain. Okay, who am I going to see first?" she asked.

"Ashley," Brent said. "She's worse than me."

"Fine. Can you get up on my examination table, please?"

Ashley went over to the table and as she climbed up she let out a little whimper of pain. The doctor was looking at some papers—the papers the receptionist had drawn up.

"So your ribs are hurting you," she said. "Which side?"

"Left."

The doctor lifted up Ashley's shirt and started touching her bruised ribs. Ashley shrieked in pain as the doctor found a tender spot.

"Is something broken?" Ashley asked.

"Fractured. Two of your ribs. Maybe a third. This sort of injury is common . . . when somebody is kicked. Is that what happened?"

Ashley didn't answer right away, but then she nodded her head ever so slightly.

The doctor turned to Brent. "And it wasn't you who kicked her, was it?"

"Me?"

"No, it wasn't him!" Ashley snapped.

"Brent would never do that!" I protested.

"That's good to know. No offence . . . I just have to check. Lots of the injuries street kids have are caused by other street kids."

"They were," Brent said, "but I'd never hurt Ashley or Dana . . . or any female. I've never hit a female in my life and I never will."

"A gentleman. That's good to hear." She listened to Ashley's back with her stethoscope. "Take a deep breath."

"I can't take a deep breath," Ashley said. "It hurts."

"Do it even if it does hurt."

Ashley did what she was told and cringed in pain. "And again," the doctor asked, and Ashley complied.

"Your lungs are clear right now. No pneumonia."

"Why would I have pneumonia?" Ashley asked.

"When people have broken ribs they tend to get pneumonia because of their lack of movement and the shallowness of their breath due to the pain. Pneumonia kills more street people than anything else. I'm going to give you something for the pain—enough for two days."

"You mean it'll be better in two days?" Ashley asked.

"No. It'll probably hurt for at least a week, more likely two."

"Then why are you only giving her enough painkillers for two days?" Brent asked.

"Clinic policy. Antibiotics we give out in large supplies. Anything that's to control pain is limited to two days. There's too great a risk that somebody is going use it to get high if we give out too much," the doctor explained. "Don't take it personally. That's just the policy of our clinic. If you are still in pain after two days, come back. I'll reexamine you, make sure you're headed in the right direction, and then I'll give you another two days' worth of painkillers."

"Are you going to put a cast on my ribs?" Ashley asked.

"In the olden days they used to tape them up, but then they found out that that actually *caused* pneumonia. What you can do is use your arms to support your ribs. Wrap them around yourself like this," she said, as she sort of hugged herself. "And even if it hurts you still have to take deep breaths to keep the lungs clear. Understand?"

Ashley nodded. "Got it. And thanks."

"No problem. So, who's next?"

"Me," Brent said. He got up on the table as Ashley climbed down.

"I guess we should start with your nose . . . unless it always looks that bad."

"Not before yesterday."

She reached up and placed her fingers against the sides of Brent's nose. Gently she pushed it first to one side and then the other. I could tell that it hurt, but Brent was working hard not to show it.

"Broken, but there's not much that can be done about that. I'll get my nurse to clean it up and maybe pack it. Is it still bleeding?"

"A little bit every now and then."

"Then packing it would work. Your face is also pretty scraped up. How did this happen?"

"I got kicked in the side of the head."

"I'll get that cleaned up as well and give you some ointment to put on it so it doesn't get infected." She looked down at her papers. "I'm more worried about the inside of your head."

"He didn't kick me on the inside of my head," Brent said.

"Is he always this funny?" the doctor asked me and Ashley.

"He always *thinks* he's funny," Ashley replied.

The doctor pulled out a small flashlight. "Look at the light." She held it in front of one eye and then the other. "Did you lose consciousness?"

"Nope."

"Vomit?"

"Felt like it but I didn't."

"Good. You've suffered from a concussion. If you'd come right after the assault I would have recommended that you be woken up every two hours or so."

"I told you so," I said.

"When did this happen?" the doctor asked.

"Last night," Brent said.

"Then there's nothing else that needs to be done. You might have a headache for a couple of days. I'll give you something for pain as well. Two days' worth. I can see you both again in two days."

Brent climbed down off the examination table and the doctor turned to me. "Do I need to examine you, too?"

"I'm fine, honestly."

"I don't know about that. All three of you look like you could use a shower and a good meal and a warm place to sleep."

"Are you asking me out on a date?" Brent asked.

The doctor broke into laughter. "I think I'll pass on that, although I know a couple of places where you can get a meal tonight."

"We know all those places," Brent said. "We like to take care of ourselves."

"Independence is important," the doctor said. "And so is knowing when you need some help. I'll see you in two days. Even if you're feeling better you come back. Promise?"

"We'll be here, Doc," Ashley said.

"I'll make sure they come back," I added.

WE LEFT THE EXAMINING ROOM, cut through the waiting area, and exited onto the street.

"So," Ashley said, "how are we going to take care of ourselves for supper?"

"We've still got a few hours before dark. Maybe we can do some panhandling," Brent suggested.

"I'm hungry *now*, and my side is really hurting. I just want to sit down and have something to eat."

"Then maybe we should," I said. "My treat."

"Your treat?" Brent and Ashley asked together.

"Would twenty-four dollars be enough to buy us all supper?" I asked innocently as I pulled the money out of my pocket.

"More than enough. Where did you get it?" Ashley asked.

"Let's eat," I said. "Maybe tomorrow I'll show you how I did it."

chapter eleven

"SO, COME ON, TELL US WHAT YOU HAVE IN MIND," Brent said.

"I told you. I think I know a way we can make some money," I answered.

"Yeah, but how? Are we going to panhandle or squeegee or rip somebody off or—?"

"Get real, Brent. Can you see Dana ripping somebody off?" Ashley asked.

"I guess not . . . so . . . ?"

I smiled. "I'm not *telling* you. But I will *show* you."

I didn't know which part I was enjoying most—the fact that we were going to be making money doing art, the fact that I was going to prove to them that Sketches wasn't a waste of time, or the fact that I was finally doing something for them to pay back all that they had done for me.

We walked through the square between the big office towers till I found a good location. Then I took my backpack off my shoulder and set it down on the pavement. "This is the perfect spot."

"This?" Ashley asked.

I nodded.

"And just what makes this particular spot so perfect?" Brent wanted to know.

"For one thing, look how smooth and even the pavement is. And check out all the buildings around here," I said, pointing to the four tall, black office buildings that both surrounded and towered over us. "It's ten o'clock. In about two hours these buildings are going to empty out as thousands and thousands of people go out for lunch."

"So we *are* going to panhandle," Brent said.

"No panhandling. No lying. No begging."

I bent down and unzipped my backpack. I opened it up and pulled out a book and handed it to Brent.

"We're going to sell them a book?" he asked.

"Of course not. It's not even my book. I borrowed it from Sketches."

"It's a big book . . . a heavy book. Are we going to hit them with the book if they don't give us money?" he joked.

"I was hoping to hit them with what's *in* the book."

Brent turned it over. "It's like some kind of art book." He started flipping through it.

I reached deeper into my bag and pulled out a little whisk broom, a tape measure, a straight edge, and a package of pastels—all of which I'd borrowed from Sketches.

"I know," Ashley said. "You're going to do a copy of one of those paintings on the pavement, right?"

I took the book back from Brent and opened it to the right page. "This painting." I pointed to *Starry Night* by Van Gogh. It had worked before, so I thought it would work again.

"I think I know that one," Brent said.

"You should. It's one of the most famous paintings in the entire world."

"It's okay," he said.

"Okay? Do you know how valuable this painting is?" I asked.

"How valuable?"

"Like, tens of millions of dollars of valuable."

"Wow. Maybe I should have paid more attention in art class," he said.

"Maybe you should have paid more attention in *all* of your classes," Ashley joked.

"I guess the more important question is: how much is it worth to us?" Brent said.

"That depends on how good a job we do."

"Then we're in real trouble. I can't even draw stick people," he said.

"Me neither. I got no talent," Ashley added.

"That's okay, I have enough talent for *all* of us."

Ashley snorted. "And what exactly are we supposed to do while you're showing off all that talent?"

"Yeah, do we just stand around and watch?" Brent added.

"Not even close. The two of you ever use a colouring book?" I asked.

"Of course," Ashley said.

"Yeah," Brent answered, "but I wasn't so good at staying inside the lines."

"Well, this is going to be a lot like drawing in a colouring book, only with bigger lines." I tossed the whisk broom to Brent. "And you can start out by sweeping the pavement. Let's get to work!"

IT DIDN'T TAKE long to measure the frame, mark the main points of the painting, and start to draw. People began to take notice of us immediately, slowing down, watching us create our picture. I stood up and stepped back to look at the work in progress. The book was propped up against a pole, open to the painting I was copying.

"It looks pretty good," Ashley said.

"Not bad. I can see a couple of places where it could be better."

"I can see one way where this *couldn't* be any better," Brent said as he came over to join us.

"How?" I asked.

"Do you know how much money we've collected so far?" he asked.

I shook my head.

"Almost seventy-two bucks."

"That is fantastic!" Ashley exclaimed. "We've never got that much begging before."

"That's because we're not begging!" I said. "This is different."

"The biggest difference I see is that we're making way more money," Brent said.

"It's more than the money," I said. "It's *how* we're making the money. They're giving us money because they appreciate what we're doing, and not because they feel sorry for us or want us to leave them alone. They give us money because they think we have talent."

"*You* have talent," Ashley pointed out.

"I'm not doing this by myself. We all worked together to create something worthwhile."

"No argument there," Brent said. "So far it's worth seventy-two bucks."

"And it's going to be worth more as the day goes on," Ashley said. "The more work we do, the better it looks."

"Just wait until the end of the day when everybody comes out of the buildings to go home. We are going to make a fortune!" Brent exclaimed.

"That means we can get a great meal," Ashley said. "And maybe a motel room tonight."

"Not to mention lots of cigarettes," Brent added. "And enough to buy something else . . . something to help us forget about being out on the streets, if you know what I mean."

"I know what you mean, but I have a different idea," I said.

"What did you have in mind?" Ashley asked.

"We need to eat and have cigarettes," Brent pointed out.

"I know, but do we need to get a motel room tonight?" I asked.

"You don't want a room?" Brent asked in amazement. "You're always the one who wants a room."

"He's right," Ashley agreed. "If we have enough money, why wouldn't we get a room?"

"But what if we don't get a motel room tonight," I said, "and instead we save the money?"

"Save it for what?" Ashley asked.

"For an apartment." I'd heard some of the kids at Sketches talking about going together and renting their own place. I couldn't believe I'd never thought of it before! But then, I'd never figured I had a steady source of income before, either.

"An apartment?" Ashley and Brent asked at the same time.

I nodded my head. "Nothing fancy . . . one bedroom, or even just one room. We'd have a bathroom and a shower and a kitchen . . . we could buy groceries and cook and—"

"Who's going to rent an apartment to us?" Ashley asked.

"Isn't Brent old enough to rent an apartment?"

"Technically, but get real, who would rent a place to me?" Brent asked.

"I don't think that would be a problem if we had the rent money."

"Yeah, so where are we going to get enough money for first and last?" Ashley asked.

"First and last?"

"They only rent if you can give them the first and last months' rent in advance," Brent explained "That would take at least a thousand dollars."

"Probably more," Ashley added.

"I didn't know it was that much," I admitted. I tried to think things through, to readjust for the higher amount. "Do you think we might make a hundred and twenty bucks today?"

"Easy. I was thinking more like one forty."

"Okay, so if we spend forty dollars on food—"

"And cigarettes," Brent added.

"And cigarettes, then we'd have a hundred dollars."

"Which would leave us nine hundred dollars short," Brent said.

"But if we did that ten days in a row, then we'd have a thousand dollars, right? So we could have a place to stay . . . a *real* place where we wouldn't have to worry about being beaten up, or kicked out, or arrested, or have rats crawling all over us. We could do it."

Neither of them said anything for a while. I wasn't sure if it was because they were thinking over my idea or because they thought it was so ridiculous that it wasn't worth commenting on.

"You know," Ashley said slowly, "it would be something to have our own place."

"It would be," I agreed.

"That would be like a dream," she said wistfully.

"An impossible dream," Brent said under his breath.

"Why is it impossible?" I asked. "Why?"

He scoffed. "How long have you been on the streets?"

"You know how long."

"Do you know how long I've been out here on my own?" he asked.

"A long time," I said.

"Over two years, and do you know how many kids I've met who talk about getting a place?"

"I don't know," I said, with a shrug.

"Lots. Lots and lots. And do you know how many actually do something like that?" he asked. "Do you know how many actually get off the streets?"

"I don't—"

"It just doesn't happen," he said, cutting me off.

"Come on, Brent, that's not fair," Ashley said, jumping into the conversation. "Some people get off the streets."

"Sure, some people go back to wherever they came from, or end up in a group home or a foster home, but that's not what she's talking about. Do you know anybody who actually got their own apartment?"

Reluctantly she shook her head.

"We could be the first, then," I argued.

"What's the point in trying for something you can't get?" Brent asked. "You just get your hopes up to have them crushed."

We all stood there silently, nobody knowing what to say next.

"You kids have done a wonderful job."

I turned around. There was a man—a businessman in a suit—standing there.

"It's a real work of art," he said.

"Thanks," I mumbled.

"I really mean it. It's a shame that something this nice will only be here until the next rain."

"Sometimes the famous masters had to paint over their old paintings because they couldn't afford to buy new canvases," I said.

"I didn't know that," the man said.

"And despite the fact that the original of this painting is worth millions of dollars, Van Gogh didn't get a cent for it. Nobody wanted to buy it. He sold only one painting in his whole life."

"You're joking, right?" Ashley asked.

"He died penniless, alone, never knowing the value of his work," I told them.

"What a tragedy," the man said, shaking his head sadly.

I shrugged. It was a tragedy, but life was filled with them.

The man stood there staring at the painting. He seemed to be lost in thought. He then reached into the inner pocket of his suit jacket and took out his wallet. He pulled out a fifty-dollar bill and dropped it into the hat!

"I hope that helps," he said, "and I hope it lets you three know that *your* work is appreciated."

"It will . . . it does . . . thanks!" I sputtered.

"Yeah, thanks a lot," Ashley said.

"You three have brightened my day. Keep up the good work!" The man started to walk away.

"Thanks!" I called out after him again. "Thanks so much!"

He kept walking but turned slightly around and gave a small smile.

Brent reached down and picked up the bill from the hat. "It isn't good to leave it there," he said as he folded it up and it disappeared into his hand.

"Do you believe what that guy did?" Ashley asked.

"If I wasn't holding it I wouldn't believe it," Brent said. "That makes at least one hundred and twenty bucks today already."

"We could make two hundred bucks today," Ashley said.

"That means we'd have enough for an apartment in five days instead of ten," I said.

"It's not possible!" Brent snapped. He opened up his hand to reveal the fifty-dollar bill. He looked at it, and then at Ashley, and finally at me. "But if the two of you want to try . . . then . . . what the hell . . . let's give it a shot." He paused. "You know, the biggest problem is how we're going to hang on to the money. What are we going to do with it to keep it safe?"

"That is a problem," Ashley said. "Some people out here would kill you for a few hundred dollars."

"Maybe we could open a bank account," I suggested, and they both burst into laughter.

"We're okay during the day, especially if we stay out of back alleys," Brent said. "The problem is at night. We can't be sleeping in a squat with eight hundred bucks in my sock."

"But we can't afford to sleep anywhere else if we want to save up for the apartment," I said.

"Let me think about it," Brent said. "I'll figure something out."

Funny, I knew he would.

chapter twelve

"HEY, MCKINNON!"

I stopped and spun around at the mention of my name. Ashley stopped and turned around too. We saw Brent jogging toward us, waving an arm in the air. We waved back.

"McKinnon!" he yelled out again.

"McKinnon?" Ashley asked.

"That's my last name," I explained.

"I didn't know that."

"I didn't think Brent knew it either."

He slowed his pace down to a jog and then to a walk. He was carrying something in his hand. It looked like a bunch of papers. Not newspapers, though.

"Hello, Ashley. Hello, Dana McKinnon."

"Hello, Brent Whatever-your-last-name-is," I said. "I don't even know your last name."

"Actually, neither do I," Ashley said.

"And I don't know yours," he said to Ashley.

"That's because I never told you," Ashley replied.

"And I never told you mine." He looked directly at me. "And neither did Dana." He handed me a piece of paper and then handed another one to Ashley. I almost dropped it. I felt my legs get weak and my stomach did a flip. There on the paper in gigantic letters was my name. Under that was my picture, and below that it said "Help Us Find Our Daughter."

"I wasn't even 100 percent sure it was you, at first," Brent said. "Not until I yelled out your name and you turned around."

"It's me," I mumbled. "I have to sit down." And I slumped to the curb.

"It looks sort of like you, but not really. When was this picture taken?" he asked.

"Last fall. It's my school picture. I've changed a lot since then."

"Especially your hair," Brent said.

"Where did you get this?" I asked, finally regaining my composure enough to think of a question.

"I got the first one from a street light. It was taped up. And another one was on the side of a newspaper box. And then there are all these," he said, holding up a stack of ten or fifteen more flyers.

"You pulled all of these down?" I asked.

"No, I got them from some lady," he explained. "She said she was your mother."

"My mother! You were talking to my mother?" I gasped.

"Yeah, about thirty minutes ago."

I looked around, anxious, terrified that she was right there, that she'd see me.

"I've got to get away. I can't let her find me." I jumped to my feet.

"It's okay," Brent said. He reached out and grabbed me by the shoulders. "She isn't here. She was more uptown and headed away from here. Okay?"

I nodded my head dumbly and he took his hands away.

"What did she want . . . what was she doing?"

"Isn't it obvious? She wants to find you, and she was putting up these notices so if somebody knew where you were they'd call her."

I looked at the paper again. Down below all the big stuff there was a phone number—my home phone number—where people could call if they knew anything about where I was or how to find me. Anybody who saw these flyers, anybody who'd seen me on the street, could just call, and my mother would know . . . and my stepfather would know.

"I have to get away from here," I said.

"Don't worry, she's headed in the other direction."

"But the flyers aren't! People will see them and then call her and—"

"People barely give these poster things a second look," Brent said.

"You did."

"It doesn't even look like you," Ashley said, pointing to the picture on the flyer.

"Brent recognized me."

"But I know you."

"Lots of people know me . . . at least know what I look like, and some of them know my first name."

"None of that matters if they don't see the flyers."

"But they *will* see the flyers! You said she was posting them all over the place."

"Well, nobody is going to see *these* flyers," Brent said, holding up the sheaf in his hand.

"Why did she give you all of those?"

"I told her I'd hand them out."

"You can't do that!"

"Dana, relax," Brent told me.

"He's not going to turn you in," Ashley said, and when I calmed down for a second I realized she was right.

"I just figured that if they were in my hands they could go straight into the garbage can where nobody would see them." He stood up and walked a few feet to the large metal bin and deposited the flyers inside.

"Thank you . . . thank you so much."

"It's the least I could do."

"And we'll go back right now and take down all the ones she posted," Ashley said.

"That's right," Brent agreed. "We're here to take care of each other, like family."

"*Better* than family," I said.

"Speaking of family, I have to say, your mother seemed really nice," Brent said.

"Lots of people can *seem* nice, but that doesn't mean anything," Ashley said. "Right, Dana?"

"I guess so."

The funny thing was that my mother really *was* nice. All my friends liked her, and she never had a bad word to say about anybody—well, anybody except my father. She was the sort of person who brought home injured birds, lent money to total strangers, and did volunteer work for the Red Cross. I remembered a time when she almost always seemed happy. That was a long time ago. Before the fighting, before the separation, before the divorce, and before I started to cause problems. When I pictured her now—and sometimes she was even in my dreams—I saw her with that hurt look in her eyes . . . hurt that was put there by something my father had done—or worse—something I'd done.

I wished there were some way for me to tell her that I was okay, to tell her that none of this was her fault.

"Let's go and get those posters down before anybody else has a chance to see them," Ashley suggested.

"Sure, we can go and—"

"Not you," Brent said. "The last thing we want is for anybody to see you and those flyers together. Somebody might make the connection."

"Yeah, we'll take care of it," Ashley said.

"No, leave it to me. I don't think Dana should be alone, so Ashley, you stay with her."

"She doesn't need to babysit me," I protested.

"Yes she does," Brent argued.

I gave him a questioning look.

"He's right," Ashley said. "You're really not that okay, are you?"

I hesitated and then shook my head. I felt queasy and my legs were shaking.

"Why don't you two go to Sketches and I'll meet you later," Brent said. "Okay?"

I nodded my head, and then the tears I was trying to hide came flowing. Ashley and Brent surrounded me and put their arms around me as I sobbed.

"Hey, don't cry, kid. This is what family does. And in this family, you're the little sister, the little sister who'd be lost on her own. You *need* us to take care of you. And don't you go arguing with me about that."

I shook my head. "I'm not arguing."

"Besides, if it gets too hot for you here, if we need to, if worst comes to worst, we'll just leave this all behind and we'll head to another city," Brent went on.

"Another city?"

"We could head out to the coast," he said.

"Lots of people do that," Ashley said. "Weather is warmer. Winter on the streets here can be pretty rough."

My father was living somewhere out in Vancouver. But did I really want to run from my mother and end up getting closer to my father? It's not like he made any big effort to see my sister and me after he left. Probably the last thing he wanted was to see his messed-up teenage daughter standing on his doorstep.

"How would we get there?" I asked. We were talking about travelling thousands of miles, not hitching a ride to the mall.

"Like we do everything else," Brent said. "We'll make it up as we go along! Anyway, that's not a problem for today. What is a problem are these flyers," he said, holding one up. "Every minute we're talking is another minute when somebody could be reading one of them."

"You'd better get moving," Ashley said.

"I'll see you two later on tonight. How about I catch up with you in the arcade?"

"Around six?" Ashley asked.

"It might be later. If you can raise a little cash, get yourselves something to eat."

"We could always dip into the money we raised yesterday," I suggested.

Brent shook his head. "That's not what that money is for. Just try to scrounge enough to get yourselves a meal."

"How about you?"

"Save me something . . . if there's enough. If there isn't, don't worry," Brent said.

"We'll save you something," I said. "Whatever we get, one-third of it will be there waiting for you."

He smiled. "Appreciate it." Brent turned and started off. I watched until he disappeared into the crowd along the street.

"He really is a good guy," I said to Ashley.

"That's where you're wrong. He's not a good guy, he's the *best* guy." She paused. "At least, the best guy I've ever been around."

"He is pretty special. Did you ever think that maybe you and him . . . ?" I let the sentence trail off.

"Me and him . . . what?"

I suddenly felt very embarrassed. "You know . . ."

"Me and Brent together, like girlfriend and boyfriend?"

I nodded.

"Thought about it," she admitted.

"And?"

"And nothing," she said. "I'm not his type. Oh, wait a minute, have *you* been thinking about *you* and Brent?"

"No, honestly!" I protested.

"'Cause you're not his type either," she said. "It's not going to happen for either of us."

"Why not? I know how much you like him, and how much he likes you."

"It's more than that. I love Brent, and I know he loves me."

"Even better," I said.

"But it wouldn't work."

"Why not?" I persisted.

"I told you, I'm not his type."

"Sure you are. You're smart and funny and really pretty and—"

"And female," Ashley said, cutting me off.

"Isn't that the idea? He's male and you're female and . . . you don't mean . . . is he . . . is he gay?" I said, my voice almost a whisper, like I didn't want anybody to hear.

"I probably shouldn't be saying any of this," Ashley said.

"But he doesn't look gay," I said.

"And what exactly does gay look like?"

"I don't know," I mumbled.

"And he doesn't *act* gay either, because gay people and straight people are just about the same. Who can tell the difference?"

"Obviously not me," I apologized.

"That's okay, you're not the only one who's confused about Brent."

"Who else?"

"Brent," she said.

"But . . . but . . . how can Brent not know?" I asked.

Ashley didn't answer right away. "Look, I shouldn't have said anything in the first place so I shouldn't say anything more."

I wanted to talk about it, but there was no point in pushing. Pushing Ashley just meant getting pushed back.

Ashley looked like she was thinking. "If I tell you more, you can't talk to Brent about any of this, understand?"

"I understand."

"All right, so I'll tell you what I think. It doesn't mean I'm right, just . . . this is what I think."

I nodded.

She said, "I think Brent is gay, but he can't really admit it yet, even to himself. At least not completely."

"But there's nothing wrong with being gay," I said.

"Nothing that I can see, but you have to know where he's coming from. He doesn't talk a lot about his family, but I guess in some ways it's fair for you to know something because he already knows something about your family. He even *met* your mother."

I felt a shudder go through my whole body. For a split second I'd forgotten all about her being there, looking for me.

"Do you know anything about Brent's family?" Ashley asked.

"A bit. He's from a little town, right?"

"A little town up north. Do you know what his father does for a living?"

"No idea."

"He's a minister, a preacher."

I remembered Brent quoting from the Bible. I'd thought it was strange at the time. Now it made sense.

"Brent told me his father's church is one of those gospel churches. You know, the type where the minister is always yelling, and there's all sorts of talk about Hell and damnation and sin. Those churches are real strict. They don't believe in drugs, or even drinking, or dances, or sex before marriage, or divorce . . . or gays."

"And Brent is gay," I said.

"That's what he's trying to figure out, and he couldn't figure it out there with everybody watching. He said it was better for his father to have a kid who was on the run than a kid who was a *faggot*."

"His father said that to him?" I asked.

She shook her head. "But Brent knew what he *would* think. Funny, I doubt Brent even remembers telling me any of this stuff."

"Why wouldn't he remember?"

"He was pretty wasted at the time."

"Wasted on what?"

"You name it. Brent used to do a lot of drugs back then."

"But he doesn't do any drugs now . . . does he? Except for grass, right?" I asked.

"Nothing. He doesn't need to any more. He needed them before to try to blank out his mind so he wouldn't have to think about the things he was doing to survive."

"What sort of things?"

Ashley didn't answer.

"It's not fair to take the story this far and then just stop!" I protested.

She nodded her head ever so slightly.

"You remember how we talked about what that cop said to you . . . about how all street kids hook?"

I nodded.

"Brent hasn't done it for a while . . . more than a year . . . but when he was first on the streets he used to hustle. Men would pay him money. But not any more. He doesn't do anything with anybody. Not boys. Not girls. It's all part of him figuring things out."

"Poor Brent."

"Poor everybody," Ashley said. "But he'll figure it out sooner or later."

I didn't know what to say. I dug my hand into a pocket and discovered the supper leftovers I'd been saving.

"Can we go for a walk?" I asked.

"Depends where," Ashley said.

"Not far. Just a couple of streets over. In the alley."

"To feed that cat, right?"

"Yeah."

We started off for the alley. First we had to cross the street. I looked anxiously one way and then the other. There was basically no chance of me running into my mother, but I still looked for our car—her car. I ran across the street, dodging traffic, and didn't stop until I'd reached the safety of the alley.

"Do you think me feeding the stray cat is strange?" I asked.

"I think it's so . . . so . . . *you*."

"What is that supposed to mean?"

"I don't know. Did you ever have cat-feeding lessons?"

I gave her a dirty look.

"Don't look so annoyed," she said. "I'm just teasing you a little."

"You're always teasing me."

"Well," Ashley said, "I tease you because you're like my little sister . . . because I love you . . . you know that, don't you?"

I nodded. I felt the same way about her.

"Didn't you tease your little sister?" she asked.

"All the time."

"I wish I had a little sister, or a big sister, or a brother, or anybody," Ashley said.

"You're an only child, right?"

"Right. Although sometimes my mom made me call her by her first name and told people she was my older sister."

"Why did she do that?"

"Why did she do half the stuff she did?" Ashley asked. "I guess she just didn't want people to know she was a mother—especially not the mother of a teenager." She laughed. "In some ways she was right. She wasn't really much of a mother."

We walked along in silence for a while.

"And maybe I tease you because I'm a little jealous," Ashley continued.

"Jealous of me?"

"Jealous of the things you had. Maybe it would have been nice to have had piano lessons, or dance, or swimming, or something."

"You must have had something like that," I said.

She shook her head. "I was once in Girl Guides."

"Well, Girl Guides is kind of fun."

"I never really got a chance to find out. I only went a few times before I left the foster home and went back to my mother's place."

"I'm sorry," I said. I didn't know what else to say.

"Feeding that cat is like you because it's a nice thing to do. Who, besides you, goes out of their way to feed stray cats? And that's one of the reasons I love you."

"It is?"

She nodded and I felt all warm inside. It was nice to have somebody love you, somebody being there to help and take care of you.

"This is where I usually see Pumpkin."

"Pumpkin? You named it?"

I shrugged. "She answers to it." I cupped my hands around my mouth. "Pumpkin! Pumpkin!"

"That seems to be working real well," Ashley said.

"Pumpkin!" I called out louder. Suddenly the cat came running down the centre of the alley. "There she is!"

Pumpkin ran up to my leg and started rubbing and rubbing and rubbing. I reached down and picked her up, cuddling her in my arms. Her little motor was purring away in its strange way.

"Ashley, this is Pumpkin. Pumpkin, this is Ashley."

"Pleased to meet you, Pumpkin," Ashley said as she gave the cat a pat on the top of the head.

"She smells a little funny," Ashley said, crinkling up her nose.

"I hadn't really noticed." I put her down and reached into my pocket to pull out the chicken nuggets. I placed them on the cement and Pumpkin started to eat them.

"Chicken nuggets are her favourite," I said.

"Is that why you've been ordering nuggets for lunch and supper?"

"Well . . . I like them too. Do you know why I named her?" I asked.

"Because she's orange and a pumpkin is orange . . . I can figure a few things out," Ashley said.

"That's why I named her *that*. The reason I named her at all was that once you have a name you're not a stray any more. Pumpkin's not a stray. She's *my* cat now."

"Would it be all right if I saved her some food, too, some-times?" Ashley asked.

I smiled. "I guess there are two people who go out of their way to feed strays. Pumpkin would like that. I'd like that."

Ashley bent down and gave Pumpkin a rub. Pumpkin rubbed back against her leg.

"I think she likes you," I said. I almost felt a little bit jealous.

"You know, Dana, it's not just cats who are strays. You ever wonder about me? Why I'm out here?" Ashley asked.

"I wondered. I just didn't think I should ask."

"You shouldn't. But I'll tell you. I'm out here because of my mother," she said.

"What did she do to you?" I asked.

"She didn't do anything *to* me. It's more like she hardly ever did anything *for* me, either. She was always too busy."

"My father was so busy that there were weeks when we didn't even see him."

"What does your father do?" Ashley asked.

"He's a businessman, a big-shot executive. Some people think that careers are more important than families. I guess your mother just focused on her career."

"I've never heard being a stripper referred to as a career before," she said.

"Your mother is a stripper?"

"I guess I should say *exotic dancer*. That's what she always called it. I can think of a few other words that fit even better."

"I didn't know."

"And you know how that cop said street kids and hooking go together?"

I nodded.

"Most strippers hook on the side. Not all of them, but most."

"Did your mother?" I asked, then instantly regretted my decision. "Sorry! You don't have to tell me," I sputtered.

"I don't have to, but I will. It's not like she ever told me, but I figured she was." Ashley kept petting the cat, her eyes down, not looking at me. "She sold drugs as well, and what she wasn't selling she was stuffing up her nose."

"I'm sorry. I just didn't know."

"How would you?" she asked. "And with all the other things happening in her life she just never seemed to have any time, or interest in me. The first time I ran away she didn't even notice for a few days."

"That's awful."

Ashley looked up. There were tears in her eyes.

"At least your mother cares enough to come looking for you," she said.

"I wish she'd just leave me alone."

"You know, if you ever want to tell me your story . . . why you're out here . . . you can," she said. "What's your mother like?"

"She was . . . she is . . . nice," I said softly.

"And she spent time with you, getting you into lessons and stuff."

"She did," I agreed.

"Did she ever smack you around?"

"Never!" I exclaimed. "She never even spanked me or my sister."

"Then why are you on the run?"

I swallowed hard. "I'd like to tell you," I said, "I really would . . . but . . . but . . . I can't."

I turned and walked away.

chapter thirteen

I HELD IT IN MY HAND, turning it slowly so that the faint light coming in through the gaps in the boarded-up window reflected off the smooth metal. It went dark and then brighter as the light caught it once again. It seemed to glitter like a diamond. I turned it over and over, watching the light play against the blade. It was almost hypnotic. I touched my finger against the razor-sharp edge. I pressed the side of the blade against my arm. It felt smooth and cold. I turned it ever so slightly and the blade sank into my flesh. I watched it happen, but felt nothing. No matter how many times I'd done it I was still amazed that it didn't hurt. I drew the blade along and a line appeared on my arm. The flesh on both sides of the line sprang out and the space became dark as blood, dark-red blood. A trickle seeped out of the cut. I watched as it formed a dark line and ran down my arm and then dripped off onto the concrete.

I touched it with a finger and the blood smeared, but it still didn't hurt. It just felt numb, like nothing. Slowly that feeling spread along my entire arm and into my body and then up my spine until it settled into the centre of my head. I didn't feel sad, or angry, or scared. I didn't want to eat or drink. I didn't miss anybody or anything. I didn't have to think any more.

"Hey, Dana!"

Ashley's voice jolted me back. I quickly pulled down the sleeve of my shirt to cover the cut. Hopefully it wouldn't bleed through the material.

"Where are you, Dana?" she called out.

I folded up the knife and stuffed it into my pocket. "I'm over here!" I yelled.

"What are you doing?" Ashley asked.

"Nothing. Just thinking."

"About what?"

"Nothing really."

"That's a lie," Ashley said. "You were thinking about home."

She was right, and I was so shocked that I didn't even know what to say.

"Don't look so surprised," Ashley said.

I had spent the last few days thinking about my mother and those posters. Part of me was worried that she had been so close to finding me. Another part was upset that she hadn't tried sooner or harder. If she'd really wanted me home she could have found me . . . couldn't she? I felt so confused. I didn't want to go home, but I wanted her to try to find me. Sometimes I just wished that none of this had happened. That I had my life back—my school, my friends, a fridge with food in it, and my bed and bedroom and . . . I couldn't go back.

But could I stay here on the streets? What sort of a life was this? There was no way out. I felt trapped, with no answers, no hope.

Ashley sat down next to me and said, quietly, "You ready to tell me about your family now?"

"There's really not much to know."

"Who's in your family . . . who did you live with?"

"My mother and my sister," I told her.

"How old is she?"

"She's going to be turning eleven soon."

"That's a nice age. I remember being eleven. Grade six, right?"

"Yeah."

"Tell me about her."

I shrugged. "Well, don't get me wrong, I love her, but sometimes she can really be a pain. She's always following me around and wanting to know what I'm doing, and copying the way I dress or what I say. Funny, though, most of the stuff that she did to annoy me I sort of miss now."

"I bet she misses you, too," Ashley said. "Anybody else in the house besides your sister and mother?"

"Nobody worth mentioning," I said angrily.

"Your old man, your father, where does he live?"

"He moved out when I was ten. Divorce. I didn't see him much after that. He got remarried, had a new baby, moved to Vancouver."

"So it was just you and your mom and your sister."

"And my stepfather," I said.

"I didn't know you had a stepfather."

"I wish I didn't."

"Sounds like you don't like him much, do you?" she asked.

I snorted. "I *hate* him."

"One of my stepfathers was okay," Ashley said.

"One of them?"

"Yeah, I must have had four or five of them, and that's not even counting all the 'uncles' who would show up for a few days or a few weeks. You're lucky you only had *one* stepfather."

"Depends on the one."

"What did he do, smack you around?" Ashley asked.

"He hit me a few times," I admitted.

"He must have hit you more than a few times for you to hate him that much."

"You ever get hit?" I asked, ignoring her comment.

"Like, every day with some of them."

"And your mother didn't stop them?"

"Stop them . . . I don't think she even *noticed* it," Ashley said. "Hard to believe she could miss something like that, huh?"

"Not hard. People miss things. Nobody knows everything all the time," I said.

"I think it's more than that," Ashley said. "I think sometimes people miss things on purpose."

"What do you mean?"

"If my mother had seen one of her boyfriends hit me then she'd have had to do something—you know?—yell at him, or hit him, or kick him out, or call the police. If she didn't see it, then she didn't have to do anything."

"You think that's what happened?" I asked.

"Yeah, but—what's that on your arm?" she asked, pointing at the sleeve of my shirt.

I looked down. There was a stain showing through.

"It's nothing . . . nothing."

"It's definitely *something*. Let me see."

I tried to turn away but Ashley grabbed me by the arm and spun me toward her.

"It's nothing . . . a scrape . . . I brushed up against a nail that was sticking out of the wall," I said. I'd used that excuse more than once before at home.

"A nail?" she asked. "When did you do that?"

"Just a few minutes ago . . . just over there somewhere," I said, pointing to a dark corner of the deserted building.

"Was it a rusty nail?" she asked.

"I couldn't really tell. It was too dark to see."

"Because if it's rusty you may have to get a shot. Let me have a look. That clinic could do that, right?"

"But it's okay, I'm sure the nail wasn't rusty!" I pleaded.

"Yeah, right," she scoffed. "Rundown, abandoned old buildings only have new, *unrusty* nails. Let's have a look at the cut."

I really didn't have a choice. Reluctantly I rolled up my sleeve to reveal the gash. It had opened up and was seeping blood.

"That looks nasty. We'd better get something to clean it up and then some bandages."

"You have that stuff?" I asked.

"Of course not, but there's a drugstore a few blocks over. When Brent comes back I'll send him over to get what we need."

"Thanks."

Ashley stared intently at the cut. "This doesn't look like it could have been done by some nail sticking out of the wall. And how come your arm is cut, but the sleeve of your shirt isn't ripped?"

Before I could react, Ashley took my arm and held me firmly by the wrist. "What about these other marks?" she asked.

In the dim light I'd hoped she wouldn't be able to see the faint white lines—the scars from other times I'd cut myself. I didn't know what to say, how to lie my way out of this.

"You did that to yourself, didn't you?" she demanded.

"Why would I?" I asked as I tried to shake free of her hold. She just tightened her grip.

"Don't lie to me. You think you're the only one who cuts? I've seen girls who do this before. I should have figured it out. That's why you always wear long-sleeved tops, right?"

I nodded my head.

"Did you use the knife that Brent got for you? Is that why you didn't want to carry a knife?" Ashley asked.

"One of the reasons."

She was still holding onto my arm, and now she turned it to get a good look.

"Wait here," she said, and she got up and left the room, leaving me alone.

I felt unsure and anxious—where was she going, what was she doing? But before my mind had a chance to go in too many different directions she came back. She was holding a McDonald's bag, from supper the night before. She pulled out a clump of napkins.

"Here," she said, as she handed them to me.

I placed one against the cut and it sucked up the blood, turning wet and red.

"Press another on top," she said. "You have to stop the flow."

I did what I was told, taking a second and third napkin and pressing them down, holding them in place.

I mumbled, "Thanks."

I didn't really want to talk to her about it, but there was something else on my mind, something I needed to ask.

"You said . . . you knew other girls who cut themselves on purpose, right?"

"Yeah?"

I paused. "Well . . . did they ever say . . . did they tell you why they did it?"

Ashley sat back and took a deep breath, thinking. "I guess there's probably lots of different reasons people do the same thing. But this one girl I used to know, she used to tell me that it hurt when she did it, but it was a different kind of pain than the other hurt she used to feel." She paused. "The type you feel here," she said, touching a hand to her chest. "Inside. The pain you feel in your heart, or in your head." She paused. "She said it was like when she was feeling a pain on the outside—where she'd cut herself—she didn't feel the pain on the inside as much." Again she paused. "Does that make any sense at all?"

"Yeah," I whispered, my voice barely audible. "Yeah, it does." I knew exactly what that girl meant.

"Did your mother know you were doing this?" Ashley asked.

"Not at first. When she found out she was confused and sad. She brought me to the doctor, and then he arranged for me to see a psychiatrist and a social worker."

"And did that help?"

"I stopped cutting my *arm*," I said.

"But you didn't stop cutting, did you?" Ashley asked.

I shook my head. "I just cut on a part of my body where nobody could see it."

"And your mother didn't know?"

"She didn't *want* to know. If you pretend something isn't happening then you don't have to do anything about it. It's like you said—people are pretty good at ignoring what they don't want to believe is going on."

We both sat quietly for a while. My cut stopped bleeding, the way they always did. There was just one more thing I needed to ask.

"Ashley, that girl, the one you told me about . . . what happened to her? Is she okay now?"

Ashley just looked at me. "I'll answer your question if you answer mine," she said. "Why do *you* cut yourself?"

I shook my head. I had a pretty good idea, but I wasn't going to share it with anybody.

chapter fourteen

"SO, HAVE YOU FIGURED OUT where we're going to sleep tonight?" Ashley asked Brent as she finished off the last of her submarine sandwich. Actually, she didn't eat the final bite, the last meatball. Instead she folded it up in the wrapper. I knew where that was going. Pumpkin liked meatballs almost as much as chicken nuggets.

Brent took a sip from his drink. "Our place to sleep is in the bag."

"What is *that* supposed to mean?" she asked.

"It means it's in the bag," Brent said. "In *this* bag." And he held up his backpack.

"We're going to sleep in your backpack?"

"We're going to sleep in what's inside the backpack. Let me show you." He undid the buckles and started to pull something out—something made of nylon.

"It's a tent!" I said.

"A four-man tent."

"Where did you get it?" Ashley asked.

"Bought it from a guy for twenty bucks. A pretty good deal."

"We're going camping?" I asked.

"In a manner of speaking, yes," Brent said. "We're going to sleep in Tent Town. Although it isn't really a town, and not all the people live in tents."

"Is it far from here?" I asked.

"It's in a little triangle of land between the expressway, the lake, and a railway line," Brent explained. "Thousands and thousands of people drive by on the road or zip past on their commuter trains to the suburbs without ever knowing it's there."

"And it's okay to just set up a tent there?" I asked.

"There are lots of tents, but some other people have used scraps to build themselves little houses."

"Come on, you have to be joking."

"Nope. Little houses."

"And nobody has noticed that they're doing that?" I asked.

Brent shrugged. "It would be hard to miss, so I figure the city knows they're there. I just think nobody cares because they're not bothering anybody and they're out of sight. You know, out of sight, out of mind."

"He's right," Ashley agreed. "Nobody really wants to *help* the homeless, they just want them to be homeless someplace else, someplace where they can't see them. I hear it's not a bad place to live."

"If it's not so bad, how come we haven't lived there before?" I asked.

"It's different," Brent said. "It's not so much street kids as older people there, people who've been on the streets for years and years, even decades."

Of course I'd seen people like that around all the time. We didn't really talk to them much, but some of them seemed friendly enough. Others just seemed crazy, pushing around shopping carts filled with junk, or standing on the corner yelling at passing cars, or just plain passed out drunk behind a store or on the sidewalk.

Brent went on, "It's really like a little town, with its own rules—you know, people have to leave each other alone, no stealing, that kind of thing."

"Rules can be good," I said.

"It's one of the reasons I want us to stay there now. I never thought I'd be saying this, but I have too much money on me."

"How much do we have now?" I asked.

Brent looked around, like he was afraid somebody might overhear him, although there was nobody around us. "Close to six hundred bucks."

I couldn't help but smile. We were more than halfway there.

"You know, usually I'm not a big fan of rules—I had enough of that when I was living at home. But right now this looks like a good trade-off—a few rules for a little bit more safety," Brent said. "I gotta look out for the two of you, not just me. And I don't want anybody taking our money . . . taking away our future."

I knew what—and who—he was talking about. I didn't think I'd ever forget those punks who beat us up and robbed us. I could see those eyes, that sick smile, the evil laugh.

Brent said, "We'd better get going. It's going to be dark soon, and we have to get permission and get everything set up before then."

"Permission?" I asked.

"You'll see," Brent answered, and we grabbed our back-packs and followed him.

WE WENT UNDER the expressway, across the train tracks, and then through a small gate in a chain-link fence about ten feet high. It was an eerie scene. There were dozens and dozens of tents, maybe a hundred of them even. Although it looked as though they were all scattered about, you could see that lots of them were clustered together in little groups. Some were small, some large. A few looked almost new while others were tattered and torn and worn and looked like a strong wind might blow them away. They were green and grey—camping colours—and orange and red and rainbows, all blowing and heaving in the winds coming off the lake. The way they moved, they almost looked as if they were alive.

Interspersed between the tents were little buildings. Most weren't much bigger than the tents themselves. They were made of wood and metal—pieces that didn't belong together and had probably been rescued from dumpsters and alleys around the downtown but somehow came together to make sheds . . . shacks . . . homes. Some were just hastily put together pieces that looked less sturdy than something a bunch of ten-year-olds would nail together to make a tree fort. Others looked more solid and planned. They looked like real little houses . . . almost.

I couldn't help thinking about discarded pieces sheltering discarded people. Somehow that seemed right.

Together in pairs or clustered in groups, people stood on the strips of cement walkway—crumbling, with weeds growing up through the cracks—that formed the streets of the city. A larger group was clustered around a fire in a metal oil drum. People were laughing, joking around, talking. As we passed, some nodded in our direction, and a few even said hello. Others ignored us as if we weren't there—vacant eyes staring out at things I couldn't see. Brent was right. They were definitely older than the kids who lived in squats or slept in doorways. In fact, we were, without a doubt, the youngest people there. There were some who were old enough to be my parents, or even my grandparents.

The flaps on some of the tents were open and I caught a glimpse of people already inside. Probably tired. Maybe drunk or stoned. I heard one man talking loudly, cursing, swearing at somebody or something, imagined or real.

"Can you tell us where we can find the Mayor?" Brent asked two women who were standing and talking, each holding a paper cup of coffee.

"You'd have to go up to City Hall to see him," one of them said.

"It's that way," the other added, pointing down one of the walkways. "You can't miss it. It's right on the breakwater. I think it's two or three down from the water pipe."

"Three," the other woman said. "Big place. It has flowers out front. Petunias, I think."

"Geraniums," the first woman corrected.

She shrugged. "I was never good with flowers."

"Thanks," Brent said.

The Mayor? City Hall? What next, Munchkins with lollipops?

We started in the direction they'd pointed. As we got closer there were fewer tents and more buildings—more shacks and sheds, really. We stopped in front of a place with flowerpots filled with well-tended, blooming flowers. The pathway leading up to the door was made of crushed red stone. This place was larger than any of the surrounding buildings, big enough to have more than one room, and there was a stovepipe sticking out through the shingled roof. This guy wasn't just here for a few nights. This was his home.

"This must be the place," Brent said.

The door itself couldn't have been any more than three feet high. It made me think of the dwarfs' cottage from *Snow White*. On the door was a little metal knocker. Brent tapped it against the door three times. There was no answer.

"Maybe he's not home," I suggested.

"Maybe I should knock again."

Suddenly the door opened and a man appeared. He was older, maybe in his fifties. His hair was grey and he had a beard, but it was neat and tidy.

"What can I do for you three?" he asked.

"Are you the Mayor?" Brent asked.

"Might be. Who's asking?"

"Me . . . us. I'm Brent. This is Ashley and Dana. We were wondering if it would be okay if we pitched a tent here in Tent Town."

"Maybe you could. Why are you bothering me?"

"We didn't mean to bother anybody. We just thought we shouldn't go ahead and pitch a tent without talking to the Mayor," Brent said.

His expression became thoughtful. "Showing some consideration," he said. "Lots of kids don't understand consideration."

"We thought it wouldn't be right to just come without being invited . . . you know, it wouldn't be *respectful*." He paused. "You are the Mayor . . . right?"

He smiled. "I'm the Mayor. So, you want to stay here, do you?"

"If that's okay with you," Brent said.

"Anybody can put up a tent . . . for a night," he said. "You looking to stay for more than a night?"

"Hoping to," Brent said. "We heard this is a good place. Better than the streets."

The man laughed. "A lot better than the streets. We got order here. Rules here. Laws here!"

"Do you think maybe we could stay longer?" Ashley asked.

"Maybe. Let me ask you a few questions first before we decide anything."

"Go ahead," Brent said. "It's your town."

He smiled again, and the smile erupted into a burp—a burp smelling of alcohol. So, why shouldn't a mayor be drinking? The mayor of the city where I used to live ran his car off the road, across the sidewalk, through a fence, and into a backyard, and it finally ended up at the bottom of a swimming pool. I heard—everybody heard—that he'd been drunk as a skunk. He didn't even get charged. All he got was a chauffeur-driven car.

"Any of you ever been in prison?" the Mayor asked.

"Never!" I exclaimed.

"Me neither," Ashley said, and Brent shook his head in agreement.

"Ain't like it's something to be ashamed of," he said. "I've done my time."

I'd already noticed the crude ink tattoos on his hands. I'd seen them on lots of people on the streets. Brent had told me that they were prison tattoos. I wondered what the Mayor had done to get himself into prison.

"Might even be better if you *had* been in prison," he continued. "Rules here are pretty much the same as there. Main thing is that you stay out of people's places. Don't matter if it's a door or a tent flap. You don't go in if you're not invited. Just 'cause people don't have much don't mean they shouldn't get to keep what they have. Understand?"

We all nodded.

"Same goes for things you see lying around. Don't touch and don't take what isn't yours."

"We wouldn't," Brent said.

"Does that mean if we left something in our tent nobody would take it?" Ashley asked.

"They'd better not, unless they want to deal with the Mayor!" His eyes got dark and threatening. "How about drugs or alcohol? Any of you have any problems?"

"I don't do drugs, or drink!" I exclaimed.

"I don't care if you do or don't. Sometimes people got to do what they got to do to ease the past or the present. I just want to know if any of you have a problem that will cause the rest of us to be bothered."

"We won't bother anybody," Brent said.

"You better not. We treat each other with respect here, and that means when it gets dark we all get quiet. People gotta sleep. And nobody goes around hitting or hurting anybody else."

"You don't have to worry about that," Brent assured him.

"I have to worry about *everything* and *everybody*. That's my job. That's what a mayor does. Any of you carrying any weapons?"

"I've got a knife," Brent said.

I held my breath. Was he going to toss us out, or take away the weapons? I knew there was no way Brent was giving up his knife.

"Where is it?" the Mayor asked.

"Here in my pocket," Brent said, patting the leg of his pants. "Do you want to see it?"

"I don't *ever* want to see it. It stays in your pocket."

Brent nodded.

"Another thing. We got a curfew. The gate is locked at eleven-thirty. If you're not in by then, don't bother trying. And don't even think about climbing the fence or—"

"Hey, Mayor!" a voice yelled out. We all turned around to see three men rushing toward us. They looked to be in a hurry. They looked serious.

"He's back!" the first man said loudly.

"Good. Let's go," the Mayor said as he suddenly pushed past us.

"Should we get somebody else?" one of the other men asked.

"Why?" the Mayor asked. "There's only one of him and four of us . . . five, if you count him," he said, pointing at Brent. "You willing to help?"

"Sure," Brent said.

I had to fight the urge to ask what they wanted Brent's help with. This didn't sound like a good thing.

"Good, 'cause that's my last question. Wanted to know if you three were willing to help enforce the rules."

"Does that mean we can stay?" Ashley asked.

"You can stay for a few nights and we'll see how it goes. You follow the rules and you got yourselves a home."

A home . . . is that what this was? I guessed it was better than living in an abandoned building or under a bridge. Actually, I was willing to bet it was better than a lot of places in the suburbs that had doors and windows and fancy kitchens. Besides, this was just temporary until we got our own apartment.

"We'd better get moving," one of the men said.

"Why? You think he's going somewhere?" the Mayor asked.

"Doubt it. He went right into his tent. I just thought we should get it over with before it gets too late. We don't want to disturb people."

"Good point." The Mayor turned to face us. "It's good the three of you are here. You get to see up close what happens to people who *don't* follow the rules, who *don't* show respect to people."

The Mayor started off, the three men fell in behind him, and then the three of us brought up the rear.

"What's happening?" I hissed at Brent.

"Don't know exactly. I think they're kicking somebody out."

They stopped in front of a small, beaten-up old tent. The flap was closed, and while I couldn't see anybody inside I could see a faint light shining through the nylon.

"Harrison!" the Mayor yelled. "We need to speak to you."

There was no answer.

"Harrison!" the Mayor yelled even louder.

"I can hear you, I'm *drunk*, not *deaf*," a voice called out from the tent. His words were slurred, confirming the drunk part.

"Come on out here," the Mayor ordered.

There was no answer and no movement.

"Don't make me come in there to get you!" the Mayor yelled. His voice was angry and filled with authority.

"Don't make me come *out* there to get *you*," the man mumbled back in response. Despite it all, I had to fight not to laugh.

"You trying to make me mad?" the Mayor thundered. He had a look of pure anger plastered across his face.

"Go away! Leave me alone!"

"If that's the way you want it, then that's the way it's gonna have to be." The Mayor reached into his pocket and pulled something out. He hit a little button to reveal the glare of a shiny blade! I stepped back, almost stumbling in shock. Suddenly all three of the other men had knives in their hands too! What were they going to do?

The Mayor walked around one side of the tent and one of the men followed him. The other two went around to the other side.

"Brent?" I hissed.

"I don't know," he said, his voice cracking over the last word. "I just don't know."

The Mayor lunged forward and cut one of the tent's guy ropes. At the same instant the other men did the same. The Mayor kicked the side of the tent, causing the whole thing to collapse to the ground and settle around the form of the man lying inside. Before Harrison could even think to react, the Mayor and his men heaved the tent over, ripped the pegs out of the ground, and rolled it onto its side. He began yelling but the men ignored his cries as all eight hands grabbed the tent and wrapped it tightly around the man, who was now hope-lessly trapped and struggling inside the nylon. Then they picked up the tent and started to carry it away—started to carry *him* away!

The three of us followed after them as they carried the swearing, screaming, struggling, nylon mummy of a man. Others came out of their tents, or stopped talking and joined in until there was a parade following behind. The Mayor and his men carried their load over to the chain-link fence, which we could now see was topped by a few strands of barbed wire. Two of them grabbed the tent by the front and two from the back. They began swinging it back and forth, higher and higher. What were they going to do now? Then, as the tent reached the height of its swing, they let go and it flew up, up, and *over* the fence! It landed with a loud thud on the ground on the other side, then rolled and banged and finally came to rest against some bushes.

The entire crowd started to scream and yell and laugh and applaud. I was stunned, unable to believe any of the things I'd just witnessed. Then, before my eyes, the man started to emerge from his nylon cocoon. First his head appeared, and then he peeled the tent away, crawled out, kicked at it, and struggled to his feet. He was alive, he was okay!

"You stinking idiots!" he screamed. "You could have killed me!"

"You're lucky we didn't!" screamed back one of the men.

"You think you can get rid of me that easy?" he yelled.

"Seems pretty easy to me," the Mayor answered, to a roar of approval from the crowd.

"You haven't seen the last of me!" he yelled.

"We have—unless you're looking for something worse. You come back and it won't just be the ropes of your tent we'll cut!"

"Brave talk when you got all those other guys with you!" the man screamed, adding a few more choice swear words to make his point.

"You think I'm being brave because of these guys?" the Mayor asked. "Tell you what, you stay right there and I'll come on over—by myself—and we'll settle this for good!"

The Mayor ran forward and there was a tremendous crash of metal as he leaped onto the fence. He started scaling it—he was seriously going to climb over and get the guy!

The man bent down, grabbed the remains of his tent, and started to sprint off, running away as fast as his drunken legs would carry him. He tripped and got up, tripped again and jumped to his feet again, running away until he disappeared into some sparse brush.

The Mayor let himself slide back down the fence. He turned and walked over toward us. "You can have the spot we just cleared. And remember, follow the rules, show some respect, and you're welcome to stay. Break the rules and you'll find yourself on the outside. You'd better set up your tent now, while there's still some light."

chapter fifteen

I LOOKED OUT the front window of Sketches. The rain had slowed down but hadn't stopped. The rain was the only reason I wasn't out with Brent and Ashley creating another sidewalk chalk masterpiece. A day of rain meant we weren't raising money toward the apartment, but I was happy just the same. There was something about being at Sketches. I felt almost like I was *me*, the old me, when I was painting. Most of the time, my old life seemed more like a dream than anything real.

I stepped back to look at my painting—to *admire* my painting. I didn't think I'd ever done anything this good in my entire life. It looked like my sister and me—especially my sister. Those were her eyes, and that was how her lips curved into a smile. She was always smiling. At least, that's the way I remembered her. It was amazing how after just a few weeks my memories had started to fade.

I decided I'd better clean my brushes and go to find Brent and Ashley. We couldn't chalk today but we still had to earn money, and it wasn't fair that I wasn't doing my part.

On my way to the sink I walked past Becca, who was working on a painting of her own. We'd talked earlier, but not about what I wanted to talk about—I wanted to know what she thought of my painting. Then again, I wondered if I could handle it if she didn't like it . . .

I cleaned the brushes and went back to my easel. Carefully, I picked up my canvas and made my way over to where she was working. I stood behind her, silently, looking at her work. Her painting was a street scene—an alley, actually—I thought I even recognized the place. The painting was filled with angry streaks of red and black, and there were two small figures huddled by a wall in the corner. It was disturbing to look at. I knew people paid a lot of money for some of her paintings but I wouldn't have put this in my home if she'd paid me. It would have bothered me every time I passed by.

"What do you think?" she asked as she turned around.

I was taken aback for a split second—I hadn't even been sure she'd realized I was there, and I was even more surprised that she wanted my opinion.

"It's nice."

"Nice?" She groaned. "That isn't exactly what I was aiming for."

"Well, not *nice*. It's . . . it's . . ."

"It's what?" she asked.

I took a big breath. "It's disturbing," I said. "I don't even like to look at it," I blurted out. "Not that it isn't good, but—"

"Hey, you don't have to apologize," she said. "That's the reaction I was looking for. Do you recognize the scene?"

"It looks familiar, really familiar, but I don't know exactly where it is."

"That's good too. It's an alley, any alley anywhere in the downtown of any big city. I want it to look familiar but not to be any particular place. What about it do you find disturbing?"

"The way you used the colours, mainly. It looks so . . . so . . ."

"So what?"

"I was going to say angry, but that's wrong. It's not angry, it's sad. There's a sadness, and that's why I want to look away."

Becca smiled. "That's how most people feel—you know, people who have jobs and houses and cars and wear nice clothes. They all just want to look away. Ignore us. You ever feel like you're almost invisible out there?" she asked.

I nodded. "All the time."

"I guess that doesn't apply to me the same way any more," Becca said. "I live in an apartment and I get to eat." She paused. "Sometimes I even feel a little guilty for not being on the streets."

"You shouldn't feel guilty, you should be grateful!" I exclaimed.

"Don't get me wrong, I *am* grateful. It's just hard to go home to my nice little warm apartment knowing that a whole lot of other kids are out on the streets."

"But you're trying to help," I said. "You're here."

"I'm here, but I'm not sure how much good that does anybody."

"It does help," I argued. "It gives us hope—'cause if *you* can get off the street, then maybe we can, too," I said. "In fact, we're working on a plan. Maybe by the time the weather changes we can get a place. I mean, my friends Brent and Ashley and me. We're working together."

"That's great, because you want to get off the streets as soon as you can. You know, that's one of the things that bothers me the most. People think that kids live on the streets because they *want* to be on the streets, that they're out there because it's just so much fun."

I snorted. "Yeah, or because we think our parents are too strict, or we don't want to be nagged about doing our homework."

"You and I know better, though, right? Kids only go out on the streets because of all of those terrible things they'd face if they *didn't* run away," she said.

I suddenly felt a catch in my breath. My heart was pounding so hard that I imagined if I looked down I could see it throbbing in my chest. I had an awful fear that she was going to ask me what *I* was running away from, why *I'd* left home. But she seemed to be done with that subject.

"Let me see your painting," she said.

Nervously, I turned my canvas around and held it up so she could see it. She looked intently at it, like she was studying it, memorizing it.

"Nicki is right," she said at last.

"Right about what?"

"You really are very talented."

I felt a rush of relief.

"The detail on these faces is exquisite! Most people avoid portraits, especially self-portraits. This really does look like you." She looked at the painting again. "And who is this?"

"My sister. My little sister, Candice."

"Does she still live at home?"

I nodded. "With my mother."

"How old is she?"

"Ten . . . almost eleven. She turns eleven in two weeks."

"Do you think you'll go and see her?" Becca asked.

"I can't go home."

"Sometimes you can't. But do you know what would be the perfect birthday present for her?" Becca asked.

"For me to see her?" I asked.

She laughed. "You're right, that probably would be the perfect thing. Second best would be if you sent her a present."

I thought about that—but what could I send her, and how? I decided second best wasn't good enough for my sister. I just had to hope I would see her again, and soon.

"So when do you think you're going to finish your painting?"

"You don't think it's finished?" I asked.

"I'm sorry," Becca said. "Do *you* think it is finished?"

"Well, I don't know what more I could add."

"I don't think there's anything more you should add to the foreground, but what about the background?"

"What about the background?"

"For starters, it needs one."

"There's a background," I argued. It was really just a background colour, a mood, but I thought it was right for the painting.

"You're right, there is a background, sort of, but—" Becca stopped herself mid-sentence. "You ever hear the saying that a picture is worth a thousand words?"

"Of course."

"That's a lie. A picture can be worth ten thousand words, a hundred thousand words. It can tell a whole story. And your painting just tells part of the story."

"It does?"

"I can see part of the story on the faces of the two sisters."

I knew without looking what she meant.

"I need to know more about what's happening to the girls, the story behind them, the background of the painting. That's what will make this more than good. It'll make it *great*. I think you're capable of making this great."

"Now you sound like Nicki. She thinks *everything* is wonderful."

"You're right, she does," Becca agreed. "Me? I try never to hurt anybody's feelings, but I also never lie. If I think something's good I say so. If I think it's crap I just try not to say anything."

"So," I asked, nervously, "you really think this is a great painting?"

"No. I said it *could* be a great painting. You need to add something to make this painting more than just good. Do you think you can do that?"

"I need to think about it some more." I also needed to meet Brent and Ashley. "I'll show it to you later . . . after it's finished."

"I'm looking forward to it," she said.

chapter sixteen

"THIS IS A LONG WALK," Brent said.

"It's not that long," I argued.

"Yeah, but I should still be asleep," he said.

Since we'd moved into Tent Town, Brent had been sleeping in every morning. Ashley and I would get up quietly and let him rest. The first morning I left Ashley sitting beside the tent and went to Sketches, with plans to meet them at noon. But the next three mornings she came with me. The first time it was more that she had nothing else to do. But that morning she wandered into the pottery studio. She made a vase that first day and proudly showed it to me. It was uneven at the top and tilted ever so slightly to one side, but she thought it was beautiful. She was right. She was also hooked. And I really liked having her come along.

"So can somebody remind me why I'm *not* sleeping in this morning?" Brent asked.

"You're coming with us so you can see Dana's painting," Ashley explained.

"No, that's not it," he said, shaking his head.

"You don't want to see my painting?" I asked, feeling hurt.

"It's not that I don't want to see it, it's just that that isn't the reason I'm coming with you. I wouldn't walk halfway across town to see the *Mona Lisa*. There has to be another reason I promised I'd go."

"Is it because I told you how interesting it is at the centre?" I asked.

"It *is* interesting," Ashley agreed.

"That's not it either. Maybe I didn't really promise to come," he suggested.

"Yes you did!" Ashley exclaimed. "And don't you even try to weasel your way out of it!"

"I'm not weaseling my way out of anything."

"Quit complaining or we'll miss breakfast," I said.

"Breakfast! That's it! I'm coming because they're serving pancakes this morning! You two promised me a good breakfast and—" He stopped walking. "So why are they serving pancakes today?" Brent asked.

"It's part of their outreach program," I said.

"And what exactly does that mean?"

"It means that by serving pancakes they can get people involved who wouldn't normally come to the centre."

"That sounds sort of like a bribe."

"Don't think of it as a bribe," I said. "Think of it as an incentive."

"Well, I'm willing to eat some of those incentives and then leave."

"But what about my painting? Aren't you going to see it?"

"And my work too?" Ashley said. "My pots?"

"Did you say pot?" Brent asked.

"Oh, *har har*," Ashley answered.

"No, seriously," he said, "you actually had me genuinely interested there for a few seconds."

Ever since we'd started saving for the apartment we hadn't spent any money on anything except food and cigarettes. Brent had kept his word about that.

"Okay. I'll eat, see your painting, her pots, and then I'll leave. Do you think we can do some chalking today?"

"If it doesn't start raining again it should be dry enough by noon. It sounds like you're starting to like it," I said.

"I like earning money," he explained.

"Why don't you stick around with us at the centre until we go out?" I suggested.

He shook his head. "I have to go back and put our blankets back inside the tent in case it does rain."

It had rained hard the night before and our bedding had got wet. This morning we'd hung the blankets on the fence to dry out.

"I guess that would be smart," Ashley said. "That was really some storm last night."

"Worst I ever saw," I agreed. "Although it might have just seemed that way because we were in a tent and not a house." The wind had been so strong that I'd thought we were going to be picked up and tossed through the air.

"It was incredible," Ashley said. "Thunder and lightning and buckets and buckets of water."

The rain had come down so hard that it had formed into little streams, and one of those streams had detoured into our tent.

"This morning the guy two doors down explained to me what we have to do to stop that from happening again," Brent said. "He told me we have to dig a little trench around the tent. He said he'd even lend us a shovel."

"I like him. He's a pretty good guy," Ashley said.

"Most of the people around us are okay," Brent agreed.

We'd been living in Tent Town for ten days now. We were the only kids in the whole town. At first it seemed pretty strange—and more than a little bit scary. A lot of the people there had what Brent called "issues." But what else would you expect? People who lived in tents and shacks weren't exactly guaranteed to be problem-free.

There was the usual stuff I'd seen from older people on the streets: drugs, alcohol, and inner demons that I couldn't see or hear. Lots of people held conversations with themselves, and we'd figured out pretty quickly who we should avoid. Crazy people could get real crazy, real fast, when they thought you'd done something wrong.

Most of the people in Tent Town seemed okay, friendly, talkative. Some of them even went out of their way to be nice to us. We came home one day and the woman at the end of the row had been cooking a stew and she insisted that we join her. She said I reminded her of her daughter. And that was one of the things that I really hadn't even thought about until then. Those people hadn't always lived there. Some had families that they'd left behind . . . homes . . . jobs . . . hopes and dreams. Nobody ever grew up thinking or hoping or dreaming that Tent Town was where their life was going to lead. They were homeless people, but they were still *people*. Maybe that made it seem even sadder.

I really wanted us to get an apartment, but in the mean-time I felt pretty safe in Tent Town. Once we went to sleep I knew that nobody could get in. That locked gate was as good as the locked door of any house I'd ever lived in. Maybe better. I also knew our tent would be there when we got home and our stuff would be left undisturbed. Just about the only thing we didn't leave in the tent was our money.

We now had close to eight hundred dollars. The more money we had, the happier I should have been. Instead, I just got more anxious about somebody trying to take it away from us. There was no telling when those jerks from the alley—or other jerks who were different, but just the same—might show up on the streets. We were safe at night, but during the day, out on the streets, it was different.

Brent had seven one-hundred-dollar bills taped to the bottom of his feet—three on the bottom of one foot and four on the other. The rest of the money, in fives, tens, and loose change, was all crammed into his pockets. He said our best defence was that nobody would expect him to be carrying more than a hundred dollars. Even if they roughed him up they'd quit looking after finding the money in his pockets, figuring they'd found all they were going to find.

Brent stopped walking. "Do you smell it?"

"Smell what?" I asked, before my nose gave me the answer. I could smell the pancakes too.

Right in front of Sketches there were two long tables set up on the sidewalk, with platters of pancakes and jugs of syrup. All the seats at both tables were taken, and people were shovelling down their breakfasts as fast as they could.

"There, somebody's leaving!" Brent called out as two people got up. He plopped down on one of the chairs.

"You take the second seat," I said to Ashley. "I'm gonna go inside and say hello."

I started away, stopped, and then turned around. Brent had already grabbed a plate and was piling pancakes on top.

"Brent!" I called out, and he looked up. "You have to promise to come in after you've finished eating."

He smiled. "I'll come in, but I might not be finished for a long, long time." He reached over and grabbed one of the jugs of syrup and started to pour it on his pancakes.

I pulled the front door open just as Robert was coming out, carrying a platter piled high with more pancakes.

"Perfect timing!" he said as he walked through. "So where are your friends? Did they both come with you?"

"They did. That's Brent out there at the table sitting beside Ashley." He knew Ashley from her visits to the centre.

"I'll make sure to go over and say hello."

"Could you make sure he doesn't run away before he comes in to see my painting?"

"I'll talk to him. And that reminds me, Becca wants to talk to you."

"She does?"

"Yeah. She's inside making pancakes."

I stood there, wondering what she wanted to talk to me about. I'd finally finished the painting, and I knew she must have seen it. Did she like what I'd done, or did she think I'd ruined it? And really, what did it matter? What was painted couldn't be *unpainted*, and even if she didn't like it, who was *she* to tell *me* it wasn't good?

I sighed. Who was she? She was a talented artist whose work I admired and respected.

I walked through the studio. Partially finished paintings filled the easels. Some were good. Some were okay. Some were bad, really bad. No matter what they looked like, I knew that Nicki would have given her usual encouragement to the painter. Becca wasn't like that. If she didn't like it, she didn't lie. I'd always thought that was good. Now I wasn't so sure.

The finished works were hanging on the walls. Mine was hanging right by the . . . Why wasn't it there? Where was it? I hurried into the kitchen. Maybe Becca knew.

She and Nicki were standing over a long, flat griddle, like the one we had at home only a lot bigger. When I was small my father and I would get up early and make pancakes together. He'd heat up the griddle and we'd stir up the batter together. Then we'd search the fridge and cupboards for the strangest things we could find. Forget blueberries or chocolate chips, we'd made pancakes with peanuts, pineapple, pepperoni, and pistachios—the perfect "p" foods—or bacon, bananas, and broccoli—the "b" list—and dozens of other combinations. Some were good, some were great, others were just plain awful! I wondered, would he make pancakes with his new daughter when she got older? I hoped he would. None of what happened was her fault.

Becca looked up from the griddle. "Dana, good to see you! Have you eaten?"

"Not yet."

"Me neither. Tell you what, let me finish off this batch and I'll get somebody else to take over for a while."

"I think I can hold down the fort by myself," Nicki said.

"Thank you. Dana, let's go and talk about your painting before we eat."

"Yeah, about my painting—where is it?" I asked.

"It's in a closet in Nicki's office," she said. "Come on."

A closet? Why was it in a closet? Was it so bad that it needed to be hidden away? That made no sense. Even if

I had ruined it, the painting would still be on display some-where. Nicki liked everything.

"I've got to tell you," Becca said, "I was a little worried when I asked you to put *more* into your painting. You looked so confused, like you didn't have a clue what I meant."

"I didn't," I admitted.

Becca opened up the closet and took out my painting, propping it up on the desk. "But what you did to it," she said, shaking her head slowly. "It . . . it is just . . . just amazing."

"You mean you like it?" I asked. I'd been expecting the worst, not this.

"Like it? I love it! It is an incredible piece of art. Moving, well executed, vibrant, and troubling."

"What do you mean, 'troubling'?"

"You know how you felt you had to look away from that painting I was working on, the picture of the alley, because it was disturbing?"

"Of course." I closed my eyes. I could still see it so clearly.

"This is the same. And that's why I put it away in the closet."

"Because you didn't want to disturb anybody?" I asked.

She laughed. "The artist's job is to disturb people. No, I put it away because I think it's valuable. If you'll allow it, I'd like it to be displayed in my next show."

"You want one of my paintings in your show?" I gasped.

"I do. I sold five paintings by other new artists at my last show. I think your painting could be sold. No guarantees, and I certainly can't tell you what price it will get, but it could be sold, I'm sure. If you'll allow it . . . Will you?"

"Of course I will, no question!"

"Great. The show is scheduled for September."

"September . . . that's so far away."

"It is, but who knows, by then you might have another painting or two ready to go with this one."

"Maybe."

"It's an amazing painting," Becca said. I looked at it. "The foreground, the two sisters, is wonderfully executed, but it's the background . . . that dark, emotional undercurrent, these strong, dark strokes reaching around the edges."

"I'm glad you like it," I said. I was so happy—this was like a dream come true!

"It's just that it's so ominous, so dangerous. It's like there is something evil, and that evil is threatening to—"

"I'm really hungry!" I blurted out. "Do you think we could eat and talk about it later?"

"Sure," Becca said, agreeing with me, but looking confused. "Why don't you put it back in the closet for safekeeping and I'll go out and get us a couple of seats and some pancakes."

"Thanks," I said. "I'll be there in a minute."

Becca left the room, leaving me alone with the painting. I took a deep breath and took another look at it. It was painted with my guts and my emotions. It was disturbing . . . even to me . . . maybe especially to me. I didn't want to look at it . . . but I could sell it. Let it disturb somebody else.

"HAVE YOU SEEN BRENT?" I asked Ashley.

"Not for a while. He went inside to have a look at your picture."

"Well he's not going to be able to see it without me. It's hidden."

"You hid it?"

"It wasn't my idea. Becca said I needed to put it away . . . because it's valuable." I paused. "I was going to tell you and Brent together, but I can't wait. Besides, if he's taken off he doesn't even deserve to hear."

"Hear what?" Ashley pleaded.

"Becca wants to put my painting in one of her shows. She thinks that somebody will buy it!"

"That's fantastic!" Ashley said. She gave me a big hug. "Did she say how much money she thinks it's worth?"

"She didn't say," I admitted. "But a lot, I think."

"Maybe the rest of what we need to get into an apartment?"

"I don't know about that," I said. "And the show won't be until September. We'd better not count on it."

"So, back to the sidewalk chalk," she said. "Either way, it's your art that's getting us where we want to go."

Wow, that felt really good. And I was glad she was so confident—more confident than I was, really.

WE FINALLY FOUND BRENT in the design and technology studio. He was standing with another guy—the funny little guy who was always in there working. They were standing overtop of a motorized scooter. Brent looked up, smiled, and waved.

"Hey, girls! This is Gizmo. Have you met him before?"

"No," I said. Of course I'd seen him around, but the guys who worked in the design and tech studio didn't tend to mingle with the other artists that much.

Gizmo reached out a dirty, greasy hand for us to shake. I really didn't want to but I didn't have much choice.

"Gizmo here is a genius!" Brent declared.

I didn't know about genius, but he did have a kind of deranged, mad scientist thing going on, with his hair sticking up, thick glasses, and strange clothes.

"He made this incredible scooter," Brent said. "Tell them about it."

Gizmo started blabbering on about engine displacement and speed, gear ratios, two-stroke engines, and a bunch of other stuff. I knew he was speaking English—I recognized the actual words—but he might as well have been speaking a foreign language for all I understood.

What I saw was a motorized scooter. A very cool motorized scooter with a custom paint job. It looked as though it would be fine to ride on.

"And do you know what's even more amazing?" Brent asked. "He made this whole thing from spare parts and pieces."

"Pretty amazing," Ashley said, and I nodded encouragingly.

"And what's even more amazing is that he can put one of these scooters together out of parts that are worth less than *three hundred* dollars, and he can sell them for up to a *thousand* dollars. Isn't that something?"

"That's a good profit," I agreed.

"That's a *great* profit," Brent said. He turned to Gizmo. "Do you think you could leave so that I could talk to the girls?"

Gizmo nodded and left us alone in the studio.

"I wanted to talk to you two about something. A way to more than double our money in the next two weeks," Brent said.

"What did you have in mind?" Ashley asked.

"You've met Gizmo, and you see his scooter," he said, patting it on the seat.

"You want to *buy* a scooter?" I asked in shock.

"Not *buy* one. *Build* one. Gizmo is willing to teach me how to build these."

"That would be incredible!" Ashley said.

"It *would* be incredible . . . it's just that . . . I'd have to use some of the money to buy parts."

"Some of *our* money?" Ashley asked.

"Yeah. A couple of hundred dollars. That much is mine anyway, right?"

"But . . . but . . . we're saving to get an apartment . . . an apartment for all of us . . . we're almost there," I reminded him.

"I'm just planning for the future," he said.

"But the apartment *is* our future. Together," Ashley said. "Don't you want to be with us?"

"Of course I do . . . it's just that I'm looking farther ahead. I have to figure out where I'm going to be, what I'm going to do. Even after we get the apartment we're going to have to keep making the rent, plus money for our food and other expenses. I have to do something . . . I don't want to end up right back on the street, with no way to make a living except scrounging for cash."

"But it sounds like you're telling me it's a choice between our apartment and you taking a chance on this scooter business, and I think—" Ashley began.

"Can't we do both?" I asked.

They both looked at me.

"We just keep saving. If we can save a thousand we can save twelve hundred. So we stay at Tent Town a week or so longer. There are worse places to be."

They both thought for a moment, then nodded their heads in agreement.

"Deal?" I asked.

"Deal," Ashley said.

Brent reached over and wrapped one arm around me and the other around Ashley and pulled us close.

"Thanks for understanding. This will all work."

"As long as we work together," I said, "I think we can all have what we want."

chapter seventeen

I WAS STARTLED AWAKE by the sound of a loud, angry engine, shattering the quiet of the night. What could that be? You'd think, living by the expressway in the middle of a city, I'd get used to loud noises, but they still bothered me. The engine roared again. This was *really* loud. So loud that I could almost feel the ground shaking underneath me. It sounded like a truck. An *enormous* truck just outside our tent.

"I can't sleep with all that racket," Brent said, his voice barely audible over the rumbling outside. I wasn't surprised that he was awake—how could anybody sleep through that noise?

"It sounds awfully close," Ashley said, poking her head out from under her blanket.

"It'll go away," Brent said. "Just roll over and go back to sleep. It's not time to get up yet."

He was right. There was barely any light coming in through the nylon of the tent, so it was still before sunrise . . . sunrise happened around six in the morning. I wondered what time it was, but there was no way I could make out the dial of my watch in the dim light.

Suddenly the sound of the engine got even louder and there was an explosion—a crash—the sound of metal against metal! All of us sat bolt upright.

"What the hell was that?" Brent exclaimed.

Before anybody could think to answer, or even think about anything, the noise of the engine was punctuated by the sounds of men yelling and feet running on gravel. Then the whole tent was bathed in bright light.

"Get out!" Brent screamed.

I threw off my blanket and scrambled for my shoes as Brent fumbled with the zipper of the tent. The flap opened up and even brighter light flooded in. I looked away from the glare. Brent popped out through the opening and Ashley scurried out on all fours. I grabbed my shoes and crawled out after them. I got to my feet and then froze in place, stunned by the scene.

There were men, dozens and dozens of men. They were all wearing uniforms. Police ... no ... more like security guards. And each man was carrying a big flashlight, the beam dancing and jumping as they walked and ran. Moving down the street was a gigantic bulldozer, its lights blazing. It inched along the road. I looked past it to the fence. There was a gaping hole where the gate had stood, and the fence was mangled. That was the sound, the bulldozer crashing through the locked gate and the fence.

The security guards, in pairs, were stopping at each tent or shack. They pounded on those dwellings that had doors, hammering them with their big flashlights. Tents were unzipped, the flaps ripped open, and the flashlights aimed inside.

"Get out! Everybody get the hell out!"

Weary, confused, tired, stoned, stunned, hungover, half-dressed people crawled out of their tents or shacks and into the dim early-morning light. The sun was just starting to push its way over the horizon. The people stood in complete silence, watching the scene unfolding before them like it was a terrible dream, or a bad drug experience, or just part of the delusions that normally haunted them. It was none of those. It was real—terrible and real.

The men—the security men—started herding people forward. I felt a sense of overwhelming panic. I was desperate . . . I had to get away. I scanned the scene around me, searching for a way to escape. Past the line of security guards sweeping people along was another line of men, standing at the fence, beams from their flashlights marking their spots. There was no way out. I moved forward, staying very close to Brent, hoping that somehow he could save me, that he could protect me.

"What's happening?" I gasped.

"Isn't it obvious?" he answered.

"Not to me. Are they going to hurt us?"

"Not if we don't give them a chance. Don't argue with anybody, don't push even if they push you, and keep your mouth shut," he said.

"But what are they doing, why are they here? What's going to—?"

"Can I have your attention!" a loud, amplified, metallic voice boomed out. Each word echoed back at us off the buildings before flying out over the lake and sinking beneath the waves. I looked around, trying to search out the source of the voice. There he was—a man standing on the back of a flatbed truck, just outside the fence, a bull-horn in his hand. There was already a crowd of people by the truck and we were being herded in that direction to join them.

Just over to my side a man spun around and pushed one of the security guards. Before he could even move two more security guards materialized, knocked him down, and pinned him to the ground beneath their feet and knees!

Almost as quickly a pair of police officers were on top of the scene. Thank goodness, they ordered the security guards off the man. They helped the poor man to his feet and then they spun him around and started to handcuff him! What were they doing? He was the one who was attacked, and they were arresting *him*? The two police officers led him away, one holding each arm.

"I am here this morning," the bullhorn man shouted, "as the legal representative of Helping Hands Hardware Incorporated, the owner of this property."

He was standing high above everybody on the back of the truck. At his side were two large, burly security men, flashlights in hand. Another half-dozen guards stood by the truck, between him and the crowd.

"I am notifying all of you that you are *illegally* trespassing on private property. You are hereby ordered to leave said property—"

"This is our land!" screamed out a voice, cutting him off. It was the Mayor! He pushed his way to the front of the crowd until he was stopped from going any farther by the security guards. "And I order *you* and your *thugs* to leave immediately!" the Mayor yelled.

The crowd, which had been sullen and sleepy and silent, suddenly sprang to life and cheered for the Mayor.

"This," the bullhorn man blared out, "is the legal property of Helping Hands Hardware Incorporated and we have a court order, issued yesterday, to clear the property of all possessions and people!" He held a piece of paper above his head, like somehow waving a few words would be enough to make us leave.

"Stay close to me in case something starts," Brent said. "And if it does start, you and Ashley make sure you keep your arms and hands wrapped around your heads, for protection."

"Protection from what?"

"From getting your brains splattered all over the ground. Why do you think all those guards have those big flashlights? Those are clubs they're going to use to bust heads open if people resist," he explained. "And you can expect some flying rocks and bricks to be coming in the other direction. No telling who they might hit."

"We don't believe in you or your courts or your orders!" the Mayor screamed. "In here, I'm the law!"

"You are trespassing," the bullhorn man yelled back. "You are on our property *illegally* and you are ordered to leave within the hour."

"And if we don't leave?" the Mayor demanded. "What are you going to do then?"

"We hope you will leave co-operatively," came the amplified answer.

"We ain't doing anything co-operatively," the Mayor screamed back. "So what are you going to do?"

"You have one hour to gather your things and go. If you remain, then we will have no choice but to execute the eviction notice by *force*."

"You think you can evict us?" the Mayor yelled. He was sounding angrier with each passing word. "You and what army?"

It was obvious even to me what army—the dozens and dozens of security guards who surrounded us. I watched now as each of those security guards held his flashlight in front of him—not for light, but as a weapon. It was like Brent had said, they were going to use them as clubs. And I knew that practically everybody in the crowd had a weapon on them . . . and men like the Mayor were prepared to use them. I could see people puffing themselves up, ready for a fight, and others, like me, trying to shrink away, bracing for what was going to come.

"We have to get out of here," I hissed at Brent. "We have to get away from—"

"I want everybody to just stop!" yelled out a voice. A large police officer, stripes on his shoulders, moved past us and to the front of the crowd. The security guards stepped to the side as he climbed up on the truck and took a position beside the bullhorn man. He was big, bigger than the bullhorn man, bigger than either of the two security guards who flanked him.

"I'm Sergeant Malik, and my men and I were sent to see to the safety of the people . . . all the people," he said. His voice was so big and booming that he didn't need the bullhorn to be heard. "There will not, I repeat, *not* be any use of excessive force." He turned and directly faced the bullhorn man, who looked away.

"These people do have a duly executed court document," the Sergeant continued. "They have the right to ask you to leave this property."

"Leave it to go where?" a woman asked in a desperate voice.

"Behind you you'll notice that there are buses."

I turned around. There were four big yellow school buses sitting on the road just outside the fence.

"These buses are for your transportation. They will bring you and your possessions to one of a number of shelters where you can—"

"I ain't going to no shelter!" yelled the Mayor.

"Me neither!" screamed another.

"I'd rather sleep under a bridge than go to a stinking shelter!" came another voice.

The Sergeant held up his hands to silence the crowd. "That is your choice, and maybe I can't blame you. You are free to go elsewhere for the night, if you choose. The city and Helping Hands Hardware have also set up an emergency fund. Those of you who are eligible can receive money to spend the next week in a motel selected by Social Services until you can find other accommodations."

There was grumbling from the crowd as people discussed what they'd just heard among themselves.

"You think you and a few officers and a bunch of rent-a-cops can move us?" the Mayor asked. "There are close to two hundred of us. You gonna arrest us all?"

The crowd started to yell and scream support again. I saw two men right in front of us reach into their pockets and pull out their knives. Another man bent down and picked up a broken-off piece of cinder block.

"He's right!" the Sergeant yelled, and the crowd suddenly got a lot quieter, as though they were shocked by his reply.

"We can't arrest all of you," he continued. "Just some. Just those who are the leaders. Those are the people we're going to charge with instigating a riot. And we're also going to check everybody here and see if anybody has any outstanding warrants or charges and we're going to arrest those people, too."

Even the mumbling in the crowd now stopped.

"I don't want to arrest anybody," the Sergeant continued. "That's why I'm giving everybody a chance to just move on."

The bullhorn man stepped forward and brought the bullhorn up to his mouth. "We have also provided a meal for you. Just outside the fence you will see a large catering truck, the shiny silver vehicle. Once you have packed up your possessions you are welcome to have some breakfast."

Despite everything I burst out laughing. Ashley and Brent stared at me like I was crazy. I just couldn't help myself. It was like we were some sort of stupid animals and we could be tricked into leaving our homes by the promise of a little bit of food.

"We need people to start gathering up their things," the bullhorn man said. "In one hour the construction crew will be arriving to start preparing the site . . . in one hour."

"Take as much time as you need!" the Sergeant called out. "If you need a few hours, take it, and remember we're here to make sure that everybody follows the law . . . *everybody*." I knew he wasn't just talking to us but to the bullhorn man and the security guards as well.

We were going to have to leave. What choice did we have? What choice did we ever have?

I SAT ON THE GROUND, my back against the bridge abutment. A paper plate, now half emptied of the gigantic second helping of bacon and eggs I'd gotten, was balanced on my lap. It had been almost two hours since they'd first arrived, and the last few stragglers were being herded out of the gate. In the end, most were leaving quietly. A few—the Mayor and some men like him—had put up some resistance, but even they realized there was no point in fighting. A couple of men, drunk or stoned, were too out of it to either co-operate or resist and they were taken away. One woman, ranting and raving and screaming about the CIA and aliens, was removed as well. They said they were going to take her to the hospital. Somebody should have taken her there a long time ago.

A second bulldozer and three large trucks, filled with construction workers, had appeared on the scene. Many of the workers were busy with the fence that surrounded the property. They were mending holes and fixing the gate, smashed open by the bulldozer first thing that morning. In addition they were stringing up more barbed wire along the top of the tall fence. It was obvious that once we were all on the outside they were going to try to keep us from getting back in.

There was a loud crash, and a puff of dirt and dust flew up into the air. Brent jumped to his feet to see the source of the sound.

"It's the Mayor's place," he said. "They just ran it over. It's gone, flattened by the bulldozer."

Ashley got to her feet to look as well.

I didn't get up. I closed my eyes. I didn't want to see.

"HOME SWEET HOME," Brent said as he kicked in the board that was blocking the window. He reached down and wiggled it until the nails came free and he pulled it off the window frame, tossing it across the alley.

He reached into his pack and pulled something out. It was a flashlight . . . a long, black flashlight like the ones all of those security guards had.

"Do you like it?" Brent asked. "I *found* it this morning . . . I don't know where it came from," he said, and started to laugh.

He aimed the light into the building and the powerful beam cut through the deep darkness, creating a path for us to follow. He climbed in through the window and I followed. It was awkward to manoeuvre through the small opening with my pack still on my back. It was filled with all my things, including two blankets and a small pillow— things we'd accumulated at Tent Town. The tent was now gone. Brent had sold it for thirty-five bucks to a couple of guys whose shack had been flattened by the bulldozers. They said there was a spot down by the river where they were going to set it up. We wished them luck and pocketed the money.

Some of our Tent Town neighbours were in motels tonight, courtesy of Social Services, but we figured they'd have taken one look at us and started checking us against their list of runaways, and we didn't need that. Better to just slip away quietly and make our own plans, as usual.

"Have we been here before?" Ashley asked as we moved slowly across the floor of the deserted warehouse.

"I've been here before. Maybe before your time," he said. "There's a good place to sleep in the corner. It's sort of protected and nobody comes here . . . at least not very often . . . so we won't be bothered."

I hadn't even thought about that. In Tent Town we were safe. There were rules. There was the Mayor. Here we were on our own again. I reached down and felt the knife in my pocket. Maybe I really did need to have a weapon.

"This place really smells bad," Ashley said.

"Squats don't usually have air-fresheners. You just got used to the fresh air coming off the lake."

"It was nice. Maybe we shouldn't have sold our tent," I suggested.

"A tent is no good unless you have a place to pitch it. A safe place," Brent said.

"Some people said they were going to try to set up another Tent Town, make it even bigger and call it Tent *City*," I said. "When that happens, maybe we can buy another tent and—"

"*If* that happens," Brent said, cutting me off, "it's not going to be for a long time, and by that time we'll be in our apartment."

"I like it when you talk that way . . . like there's no doubt," I said.

"There is no doubt. It's happening," he said. "And it's happening because of you."

"Me? We've all been working, and saving."

"But it was your idea, and without that idea nothing would have happened."

"He's right, Dana," Ashley agreed.

"So remember, this is just temporary. We'll only be here or someplace else for a few more nights . . . a week . . . maybe two at most."

"I'd rather it was someplace else," Ashley said. "This place really does stink!"

I didn't think any squat smelled nice, but I had to agree. There really was a thick, foul stench in the air.

"You've both been spoiled," Brent said.

"You have a head cold or you'd smell it too," Ashley countered.

"Quit complaining. It's through this way." Brent pushed open a door and we were greeted by a wave of foul-smelling odour that practically threw me backwards.

"Whoa, now even I smell it!" Brent agreed.

"What could possibly smell that bad?" I asked.

Brent started to shine the flashlight around the room. Slowly the beam revealed garbage and bits of wood and broken concrete, and then it stopped moving. There was something on the floor in the corner. It was a lump, a mound, a person-sized object beneath an old tattered blanket.

"Somebody's here," I whispered. How could he stand the smell?

"Hello!" Brent called out.

There was no answer. No movement.

"Must be sleeping," Brent said.

"Or stoned," Ashley added.

"Hello!" Brent yelled, and I practically jumped off the ground, startled by his voice. There was no response.

Brent edged forward. I wanted to stay put or even run in the opposite direction but I found myself moving with him, unable to resist, maybe too frightened to separate from him even a few feet.

"Hello!" Brent called. "Are you okay, buddy?"

Still no response. We continued to move forward. It was definitely a man, a person, lying beneath the blankets right at our feet. The smell was overpowering; my eyes started to tear up.

"Hey, buddy," Brent said. No answer.

Brent reached out a foot and gently nudged the man. Nothing. He put his foot against the man's side and pushed. The man rolled over and the light revealed a rotting, insect-infested face with empty eye sockets staring up at us! I screamed and felt myself starting to faint, and then Brent's strong arms wrapped around me and I stumbled away.

chapter eighteen

"DANA, IT'S OKAY," Ashley said as she squeezed me even tighter in her arms.

I continued to sob. Loud, deep sobs that started in my chest and worked their way up my throat and out. I'd tried to stop crying but I couldn't. I'd tried to stop shaking but I couldn't do that either. At least I'd stopped throwing up. Three times between leaving the warehouse and reaching the coffee shop I'd had to double over and puke.

"You've got to stop," Brent hissed. "People are staring."

I raised my head from Ashley's shoulder and gazed around. There were about two dozen people sitting on the stools at the counter or clustered around the little tables. Some were staring at their coffees. Others were looking directly at us.

"Just take a sip of coffee," Brent suggested as he pushed a paper cup across the table toward me.

Ashley loosened her grip and I reached for the steaming cup of coffee. My hand was shaking badly. I used both hands to pick up the cup and brought it slowly to my mouth. Before I took a sip I inhaled deeply the strong aroma of the coffee, hoping to replace that awful stench that seemed to cling to me still.

I took a sip. It was hot and sweet. Usually I didn't drink coffee this late at night—it was after midnight—because it kept me awake. Tonight it didn't matter because whatever I did or didn't do, I wasn't going to sleep. I didn't even want to close my eyes, because every time I shut them I saw that face. I shuddered and started to shake again. I took a deep breath to suppress the sobs.

"How old do you think he was?" Ashley asked.

Brent shrugged. "Hard to say, you know, because of what his face looked like, but I think he was old . . . maybe thirty or even forty or fifty. I would have a better guess if I'd had more time."

We'd rushed out—a mad run with me screaming and tripping and falling down and getting back up and tearing through the dark warehouse. Ashley had finally grabbed me, and then she and Brent had walked me out, one on each side, supporting me so I wouldn't topple over, my legs weak and wobbly and unable to hold me up.

"What do we do now?" I asked.

"Finish our coffee and find some place to crash for what's left of the night," Brent said.

"I meant about him, about the man."

"I don't think there's anything we can do for him."

"But we have to do something," I pleaded.

"There's nothing we can do that'll make any difference for him. He's dead and he's going to stay dead," Brent said, his voice barely a whisper.

"How long you figure he's been dead?" Ashley asked.

I looked around again, hoping nobody could hear what we were saying. They'd all gone back to their coffee and dough-nuts and weren't even looking at us now.

"Don't know. A while. A couple of days . . . maybe a week."

"But shouldn't we call the police?" I suggested.

"That won't make him any less dead. All it can do is get us in trouble."

"How will it get us in trouble?"

"Think about it. We live on the streets, and you're under-age. You don't think the police are going to ask some questions that we can't answer? Maybe even think that it was us that did it?"

"We didn't do anything except find him. We didn't do anything wrong!"

"Of course we did. First off, we were trespassing on private property. Second, we're kids living on the street, so as far as everybody in the whole world is concerned we're *always* doing something wrong. The cops would probably hold us, you know, put me in jail and hand you two over to Social Services, until they sorted out the whole thing . . . how he died."

I hadn't even thought of that. "How *do* you think he died?"

Brent shrugged. "Could have been anything. Maybe he overdosed, maybe he was sick. Maybe somebody stuck a knife into him. I don't know, and I don't want to find out. I just want to keep some distance between that body and us."

"I understand," I said. "It's just . . . it's just that it doesn't seem right to leave him there."

"Somebody else will find him, I'm sure, eventually."

"Maybe other people have found him before and just left him," I said.

"She's right," Ashley said. "It seems wrong not to do something. Poor guy deserves something more."

"At least if they found him they could tell his family what happened to him," I added.

"Maybe he doesn't even have a family," Brent said.

"Everybody has a family," Ashley said.

"Maybe he doesn't have a family that gives a damn about him," Brent said. "Maybe nobody cares if he's dead or alive. You know what it's like to have a family like that!"

Ashley looked hurt, like Brent had reached out and struck her. I guess in a way he had.

"Maybe nobody does care," I agreed. "But maybe they do. Either way, I'd want my family to know."

Brent got up abruptly from the table. "We have to get out of here," he said, as he took his cup and paper plate and stuffed them in a garbage can.

"Let me finish my coffee," Ashley said.

"Take it with you. This isn't a good place for us to be. A coffee shop in the middle of the night—how long before some cops drop in for their nightly fix of caffeine and doughnuts?"

I hadn't even thought about that. Both Ashley and I got up. I took another sip from my coffee and tossed the rest away. Brent was already at the door, holding it open. We hurried over to catch him, leaving the light and warmth of the coffee shop behind as we went out onto the street.

"We can't call," Brent said. "I understand what you two are saying, but we have to think about us. Even if we did call, anonymously from a pay phone, it wouldn't do any good. The cops would just think it was a crank call and they wouldn't even bother going to investigate."

"I guess you're right," Ashley agreed.

"Of course I'm right. Besides, we have bigger problems. We have to get off the street. It looks like it's going to rain. We have to find a place to crash tonight."

"How about if we can let the police know about the body without us having to make the call?" I asked.

"What do you have in mind?" Brent asked.

I had an idea. I just didn't know if she'd go for it, and even if she did, I didn't know if it would work.

"Well?" Ashley asked.

"Do you two trust Nicki?" I asked.

"She's never done nothing to make me *not* trust her," Brent said.

"Me either," Ashley agreed.

"Then maybe I could make a phone call. She gave me her card. It has an emergency number. She said if ever I really, really needed help I could call her. I need help. *We* need help. Can I call her?"

Ashley looked hard at Brent. I knew she'd let me call. I also knew she wouldn't say anything until Brent had spoken.

"Let's look for a phone booth," Brent said.

WE WERE HUDDLED in the doorway that was the back entrance to Sketches. The overhang provided some protection against the rain, which had turned from a light drizzle into a downpour.

"Shouldn't she be here by now?" Brent asked.

"It's only been about forty minutes," I said. "She was asleep when I called, so she had to get dressed, and I don't even know where she lives. It could be far away."

There was a loud thump and I jumped. Light cascaded into the alley, revealing Nicki holding open the door.

"Get in here," she said, and the three of us hurried into the building. She closed the door and slid a bolt into place.

"Are you three all right?" she asked.

I'd told Nicki all about what had happened when I called her. My lower lip began trembling and I knew I was going to begin crying again.

"What a stupid question to ask. Of course you're not all right." She reached out and put an arm around me and her other arm around Ashley.

"Get over here," she ordered Brent. "You need a hug too."

I thought Brent might argue. Instead he threw his arms around all three of us. I felt better being in the middle of the huddle.

"Now, I want all three of you to get changed into something dry . . . you do have some dry clothes with you, don't you?"

"Probably . . . maybe," I said. "It depends on whether the rain soaked through my backpack."

"All of you check, and if you need dry things I have some clothes in the office. While you're changing I'll go and make some hot chocolate, and maybe a sandwich. Do you all like grilled cheese?"

"One of my favourites," Brent said.

"Me too," Ashley agreed.

"Dana?"

"Yeah, I guess. But shouldn't you make a phone call first . . . about the body?"

"Already done. I called a friend of mine. He works out of Twenty-two Division."

"And . . . ?" Brent asked anxiously.

"I told him where the body was. And I told him I couldn't reveal how I knew it was there, he'd just have to trust me and my sources."

"And did he?"

"He said if I trusted the people that gave me that information then he'd trust it too."

I let out a big sigh of relief. At least he'd be taken care of. That only seemed right.

"Now get changed. I'll make the hot chocolate, and then the three of you should get some sleep."

"Where?" Ashley asked.

"I'm not going to any shelter," Brent protested.

"Of course you're not," Nicki said. "The three of you are going to sleep here tonight, in my office. I have a couple of cots I can set up. They aren't great but I'm sure they're better than a lot of places you've slept before. We don't do this very often. We could lose our licence if the zoning people found out."

"Then maybe we shouldn't," I said. "We don't want to cause trouble for Sketches."

"You won't cause any trouble. Nobody is going to find out. Just go into my office, change, get out the cots, and settle in. I'll be in with the food in a few minutes."

I FINISHED OFF the final bite of the sandwich and washed it down with the last sip from my hot chocolate. It all tasted good. It all felt good in my stomach. I lay down on my cot. Ashley was resting in the second one. Brent had volunteered to take the floor, and we'd given him more of the blankets to make up for it.

"Is everybody ready to turn in?" Nicki asked.

She came over and tucked the corner of my blanket around my shoulders. It had been a long time since anybody had tucked me in. She did the same thing with Ashley.

"Now let me just get out my sleeping bag and we'll turn out the lights," Nicki said.

"Your sleeping bag?" I asked. "You mean you're going to sleep here too?"

"I'll just pull up a piece of floor."

"You can have my cot," I offered.

"Or mine," Ashley added.

She shook her head. "I'll be fine."

"You don't have to do this," I said. "You can go home. We'll be okay."

"I'm sure you will, but I also think that it might be hard for you to sleep tonight, after what happened, and if any of you need to talk, I'll be here."

I was going to argue, but she was right. It was going to be hard to sleep, and having her there would make it easier. It felt good to have somebody looking out for us—an adult. It had been a long time since that had happened, even before I left home.

"I'm just sorry I don't have a bedtime story to tell," Nicki said. "Like a fairy tale."

"That's okay," Brent said, "I never believed in those anyway."

"Well, they do have a whole lot of strange and magical stuff in them," Nicki agreed.

"That's not the part I don't believe in," he said.

"Then what is?" she asked.

"The last line of all those stories," he said. "You know, the one that goes, 'And they all lived happily ever after.'"

chapter nineteen

WE'D GOT UP, put away the cots, put our stuff back in our packs, and eaten a breakfast of day-old bagels and juice in the kitchen. None of us was in any hurry to leave. I had a new painting I was working on, and Ashley wanted to try another pot, and shortly after the place opened Gizmo showed up and he and Brent started working on one of his scooters. They had agreed to work on the next one together—that one was going to be Brent's.

We didn't go out to panhandle, or to eat, or even to take a breath of fresh air. A couple of times Brent and Ashley stepped outside for a smoke, but I got the feeling that neither of them wanted to venture more than a few feet away from the entrance. It was like we were all feeling scared and vulnerable, and the building was keeping us safe.

I heard a ripple of conversation and turned around to see what everybody was staring at. There were two men—two guys in suits and ties—standing at the door. Even though they weren't dressed in uniforms, it was obvious they were cops. Cops always looked like cops. Nicki saw them and walked toward them.

"Good afternoon, gentlemen. Can I help you?" she asked.

"Yes, we're looking for a Nicki Fullerman," the first cop said.

"That's Fuller*ton*, and that's me."

"Sorry, that's the way it's written down," he apologized. They introduced themselves to Nicki and shook her hand. "Is there somewhere we can talk . . . privately?"

"Certainly. Let's go to my office."

I watched them go. Nicki ushered them into her office, and then, just as she was about to close the door, she gave me a reassuring nod, as if to say, *Don't worry, it will be okay.* I understood what she was silently saying, even if it wasn't very reassuring.

I turned away and tried to focus on my painting. I picked up the brush and realized that wasn't going to happen. All I'd do by trying to work on it now was ruin it. It was a painting of Pumpkin sitting all puffed up on the edge of a dumpster. I put down the brush. I had to talk to Brent and Ashley, let them know what was happening.

First I went into the design and tech studio. Brent and Gizmo were working away on one of the scooters. They were both so absorbed in their work that they didn't even notice me enter the room. I cleared my throat. Nothing. I cleared it more loudly, and Gizmo looked up. He smiled. He was a strange little guy, but nice.

"Hey, Dana, how's it going?" he asked.

"Good. Can I speak to Brent for a minute?"

"Sure. Brent, how about if I take over with that?" Gizmo suggested.

Brent got up off the floor, grabbed a rag, and wiped his hands, which were now almost as filthy as Gizmo's.

"Do you want to hear about Giz's latest idea?" Brent asked.

"Sure, but could I tell you something first?"

"It's really a great plan," he said, ignoring the second part of what I'd just said. "You know those guys who sell nuts and popcorn on the streets? Well, did you ever wonder where they get those popcorn contraptions from?"

"I've never really thought about it," I said. They were a strange sort of combination of popcorn-popper and glass case built on a bicycle that they rode through the streets to get to where they were going to set up and sell.

"Well, I don't know where they get them from either," Brent said, "but Gizmo thinks he can make them, and it wouldn't cost a lot of money."

"Less than two hundred dollars each if we can scavenge the parts," Gizmo said. "And we could sell them for a lot more than that."

"A *lot* more. That is, if we wanted to sell them," Brent said.

"But why would you make them and not sell them? Is Gizmo planning to sell popcorn?"

"Not him," Brent said. "Other people."

"What other people?"

"People who want to make some money," Gizmo said.

"We could rent them to kids, kids like us, who are on the street. They could go out and sell popcorn and nuts and then give us a cut of the profits for using the gear. Think about it, they could earn money, really earn money and not just beg or steal it. They'd be able to have a job, and we could make money too. It would be a business."

"That's . . . that's . . . an incredible idea!" I exclaimed.

"And just think," Gizmo said, "it wouldn't just be a better way for a few people, this could be a way that a lot of people, a lot of street kids, could benefit. It's a way of giving back . . . the way we're supposed to give back here at Sketches."

"That's really great," I said.

"Now, you wanted to tell me something?"

"Yeah." I looked around the room. There was nobody there but Gizmo and Brent and me.

"We can talk." Brent must have known what I was thinking. "Don't worry about the Giz, here."

I hesitated for a second and then started. "There are a couple of cops here at the centre."

"There are cops here all the time," Gizmo pointed out.

"Yeah, but these guys aren't beat cops in uniform," I said. "They're in plain clothes, and they asked to speak to Nicki, and they went into her office and closed the door."

"Then we'd better get out of here, now," Brent said.

"Do you think they're here about the body?" Gizmo asked.

I did a double take. How did he know about that?

"I told him," Brent said. "I know we agreed that we weren't going to tell anybody, but I trust him. You know, trust him like a partner."

"I won't tell anybody," Gizmo promised. "Do I seem like the type of guy who goes blabbing things around?"

I shook my head.

"So you think they're questioning Nicki?" Brent asked.

"What else?"

"You have nothing to worry about. Nicki won't sell you out. Not her style," Gizmo said.

"Even if she doesn't say anything, though, the cops have probably figured out that somebody she knows through

Sketches told her about the body. Maybe even somebody who's here today."

"Let's not take any chances," Brent said. "Let's get out of here."

"You're better to stay," Gizmo said. "You leave and it only draws attention. Cops are kind of like dogs. They chase whoever is running."

He was right again. I quickly thought of the number of kids who were in the centre today. There had to be twenty or twenty-five people. Too many for them to know that it was Brent or Ashley or me, but few enough that they might start asking questions and maybe figure it out.

"Where's Ashley?" Brent asked.

"She's in the pottery studio."

"Does she know about the cops?"

"I don't think so. I was going to talk to her after I talked to you."

"You should go and tell her now. Whatever we do, none of us should go anywhere near Nicki—especially not you."

"Why especially me?"

"Because you're underage, and we've got to assume your mother passed out those posters to the cops," Brent said.

That thought sent a chill up my spine. I'd forgotten about my mother and the posters. I wasn't even thinking about being a runaway. I thought about the way I'd stared at the cops when they came in and then watched them file into Nicki's office. They hadn't noticed me; they hadn't even looked in my direction.

"I'll go and talk to Ashley," I said, and started to walk away.

"Oh, one more thing," Brent called out after me. I stopped. "You can also tell Ashley that the three of us won't be sleeping under any bridge tonight. We have a warm, dry floor where we can lay out our stuff."

"We do?"

"Yeah, Giz's place."

"You have a place?" I asked.

"It isn't much. I rent a room on the top of a garage, but it's dry and warm. It even has a sink and a hotplate."

"Does it have a bathtub?" I asked.

"It doesn't even have a toilet," he said. "Sorry."

"No, that's okay, I'm sorry for even asking," I said. "Thanks for letting us stay with you, we're really grateful . . . *I'm* really grateful. Thanks."

"Hey, what are friends for? Besides, sometimes it's lonely living by myself. It'll be nice to have people around."

I smiled. It *was* nice to have people around, especially people you could trust.

"And you're welcome to stay until you save up enough money for your apartment," Gizmo said.

"Are you serious?"

"Completely."

I felt like throwing my arms around him, but I really didn't know him that well. What the heck? I went over to him and gave him a big hug. He looked shocked.

"That's okay, no problem," Gizmo stammered. It looked like he was blushing.

"I'd better go and talk to Ashley. Can I tell her about staying at Gizmo's as well?"

"Sure. Always best to give some good news with the bad."

I left them to work on their scooter and went into the pottery room. The big kiln in the corner was fired up and was baking some clay. It threw heat clear across the room.

Ashley was one of six kids working with one of the local artists who used the centre. She was at one of the pottery wheels, "throwing" a pot. I walked over until I stood right overtop of her. She looked up briefly, smiled, and then refocused on her work. Her hands were on a piece of clay that she was shaping into a tall, tall vase. She pumped one of her feet to power the wheel and it spun at an incredible rate, sending little splashes of clay-coloured water to splatter her arms and apron.

"It looks nice," I said.

"It's getting there," she said, "but every time it gets close to where I want it, tall and thin, it just tips over or tears or—*aaaaahhhh*!" Ashley screamed as the whole top of the vase came off in her hands and the rest collapsed onto the wheel.

"That's the third time that's happened! I give up!"

"It's a little early to give up," the instructor said. "But it is time to take a break. How about you go out for a smoke and then come back and try again."

"The smoke I agree with, but the trying again part I'm not so sure about," Ashley said as she got to her feet.

The instructor smiled. "You know you'll be back."

Ashley broke into a grin herself. "You want to come out with me while I have a smoke?" she asked me.

"Yeah. I want to talk to you."

Ashley gave me a worried look. "Sure, let's go."

We walked out of the clay studio and into the main studio area. The door to Nicki's office was still closed. Whatever they were talking about was taking a long time. We walked out the front door.

"Could you do me a favour?" Ashley asked.

"Sure."

"Could you go into my back pocket and grab my cigarettes, please?" Her hands and arms were stained with the brown of the clay.

I dug into her pocket and pulled out her cigarettes and a package of matches. I put a cigarette in her mouth, lit a match, and held it to the end of the cigarette. She inhaled, and the tip of the cigarette came to life. I shook the match and dropped it on the ground, stepping on it to put it out.

"I should probably give these up," Ashley said.

I gave her a fake shocked look.

"They're not good for your health, you know," she continued.

"*I* know that. I just didn't think I'd ever hear *you* say that."

"Who knows?" she said. "Maybe I'll quit smoking and use the money I'm saving to take piano lessons, or a dance class . . . I know hip hop lessons would do me a world of good." She started laughing, and I couldn't help but laugh along with her.

"So, what did you want to talk to me about?" Ashley asked.

"There are cops, two of them, talking to Nicki."

"About the body?"

"I don't know for sure, but I think so. Why else would they send over two plainclothes cops? They've been in there for a long time."

"Do you think she'll tell them anything?" Ashley asked.

"She might tell them a lot of things, but I don't think she'll tell them about us."

"Then we just have to keep our heads down and wait for them to leave." Ashley took the cigarette from her mouth and tossed it to the ground. She'd hardly smoked it at all. "You want to do a pot?"

"Me, make a pot?"

"Yeah. Your easel is right up front. The pottery studio is in the back and out of sight."

"I wouldn't know what to do."

"Just watch what I do and I'll talk you through it," she said.

"Maybe I should watch you so I can figure out what *not* to do. It didn't look like you were having much success in there just now," I joked.

"Not with that vase. I was trying something really hard. I'll show you how to do something easy."

"I have a few more things to tell you," I said. I was looking forward to telling her about us staying at Gizmo's place.

"Tell me inside, in the studio. I don't want to be here when the cops come out. Come on, let's go."

chapter twenty

"THAT'S QUITE IMPRESSIVE."

I looked up at Nicki. I hadn't seen her enter the room.

"You're impressed with *this* pot?" What could she possibly see in the hunk of clay I had spinning around on my wheel.

"That thing is a pot?" she asked.

"Yeah," I said defensively. It wasn't much, but after all it was *my* misshapen hunk of clay that was supposed to be a pot.

"You have to admit that it's a pretty sorry excuse for a pot," Nicki said.

"Hey, I thought you were supposed to say nice things about everybody's work!" I exclaimed.

"I'm supposed to be positive," she said. "Nobody said I had to lie." She and Ashley both burst out laughing at me and my sad little clump of pot.

"Then just what are you so impressed with?" I asked.

"The fact that you have more clay on your arms, face, and apron than you have on the wheel." And they laughed even harder!

She was right, I was filthy. I'd had trouble centring the clay and it had flown off the wheel a couple of times, landing in my lap. And then the water I'd been using to smooth it out kept spinning and spitting at me. I was wet and covered with clay.

"How about if you two get cleaned up and we'll talk," Nicki suggested.

"Will it be a long conversation?" Ashley asked.

"Shouldn't take too long."

"'Cause I was planning on working for a while longer, so it probably makes sense for me not to get cleaned up," Ashley said.

"*I'm* getting cleaned up," I said. "I think I'm finished with pottery . . . for life."

"I was just kidding around," Nicki said. She actually sounded kind of worried, like maybe her comments had driven me away from the pottery wheel.

"I know. I'm just joking too. I'll try again . . . some time . . . but not today." I paused. "Are they gone?"

She nodded. "And you have nothing to worry about. I didn't tell them anything, although they were very persistent. They took a big chunk out of my day. I have places to go and things to do."

Nicki looked at the instructor and the two other participants working away at the front. "Excuse me, I don't mean to be a bother, but do you think you three could take a break so we could have a little privacy?"

"No problem," the instructor said. The two kids quickly rinsed their hands in the sink and they left, closing the door behind them, leaving the three of us alone.

"I'll talk while you're getting cleaned up," Nicki said.

I took my hunk of clay and tossed it into the big bin with all the other unused clay. My shapeless lump didn't look much different from the clay that had never been used.

"The two officers, detectives, wanted to know who had told me about the body," Nicki began. "They even threatened to charge me with obstruction of justice, but they were just bluffing, trying to scare me so I'd give them names."

"And you didn't, right?" Ashley asked.

"Of course I didn't. I don't scare that easily. I told them that who told me wasn't important and that I'd given them all that I had. Then I turned the tables and started to ask them questions."

"What sort of questions?" I asked.

"I wanted to know about the dead man."

"And did they tell you about him?" Ashley asked.

"Not at first, but then they figured if they answered my questions I just might answer theirs."

"What did they tell you?" I asked.

"His first name was James. They wouldn't tell me his last name. He was fifty-four years old and had been living on the streets for a long time. I think I might have known him."

"You did?" Ashley questioned.

"After a while you get to know everybody on the street. It isn't that big a world. They thought he'd been dead about seven days."

I thought back to the insects eating away the man's face.

"And do they know how he died?" Ashley asked.

"They didn't find any evidence of foul play. There was no evidence of a gunshot or a stab wound or a beating. It could have been a drug overdose—they won't know until they get the lab results from the autopsy—but they think that it was probably natural causes, like a heart attack, or pneumonia, the sorts of things that street people die from all the time."

"That's sad," I said.

"So after the police realized that I wasn't going to give them any more information, they lost interest and left," Nicki said. "Although they might be back, the only thing you two have to worry about is getting the clay stains off your skin."

"It is tough." I was working hard at the sink to wash off my hands and arms, and I continued to lather and scrub away.

Nicki walked over. "What you need to do is really give them a good scrubbing with a brush or—" She stopped mid-sentence. She was staring at my arms. The crisscrossing scars seemed to shine bright against the rest of my skin. It was like the clay couldn't stain the scars the same way.

I started to lower my arms to try to hide them but Nicki reached out and grabbed hold of one of my wrists. I tried to pull my arm free, but she held on, tightening her grip. She turned my arm and examined the marks closely. When she looked up at me, I looked away. Finally she let go of my wrist and I pulled away and quickly rolled my sleeves down.

Nicki turned to Ashley. "Do you think you could leave us alone for a minute?"

"Dana?" Ashley asked.

"It's okay," I said, nodding my head, my eyes still trained on the ground.

"I'll be just outside." I heard her footfalls against the floor and then the sound of the door closing. I didn't look up.

"I'm sorry for grabbing you like that," Nicki said. "I shouldn't have done it."

"That's okay," I mumbled.

"How long have you been cutting yourself?"

I took a deep breath. "A while," I mumbled. "A couple of years."

"So, a long time before you started running."

"A long time," I agreed.

"And have you been doing it lately?"

"Just once . . . on this arm," I said, moving my left arm slightly.

"Can I look?" Nicki asked.

I wanted to say no. Instead I reached out my arm for her to see. Gently, carefully, she rolled up my sleeve and turned my arm over to reveal the scars.

"I've only done it once since I ran," I said.

"Here," she said, touching the most recent cut. It was almost completely healed but it still looked different from the others, the older ones.

"Does it hurt?" Nicki asked.

"Not now."

"Does it hurt when you're doing it?"

I didn't want to answer that. It was something very private to me, something I'd never even talked to anybody about until that day with Ashley.

"Dana, do you cut yourself any place other than your arms?"

I couldn't say a word.

"I guess that answers my question." Nicki paused. "You *do* cut yourself other places, right?"

"Yeah," I said at last, my voice barely loud enough for me to hear it.

"Those other places . . . do they include your legs . . . on the *inside* of your thighs?" she asked, touching one of her thighs with her hand.

I had never told anybody about that. Ever.

"Dana?"

I looked up.

"Am I right? Have you been cutting yourself there?"

I nodded my head, ever so slightly. "Not now . . . but before. How did you know?" I asked, my voice barely a whisper.

"I just started to put things together," she said.

"What things?"

"Come with me."

She took me by the hand and led me out of the pottery studio. Ashley was standing right outside the door. She gave me a questioning look.

"It's okay," I mumbled, and she nodded.

I followed Nicki through the main studio and into her office. I followed behind her like a little child, powerless to resist.

"I just knew," Nicki said. "I knew because of the painting."

"The painting . . . my painting?"

She nodded.

"How could you know anything from my painting?"

"It's all right there." She opened up her closet and removed the painting from where it was still being stored. She placed it on top of the filing cabinet and leaned it against the wall so we could both see it. My sister and I were staring out at us. I looked away. I didn't like looking at it.

"Sometimes I get so busy that I lose track of things. I was so happy that you did a great painting, thrilled that you had done something that Becca thought was good enough to sell, that I didn't *really* look at the painting. If it had been hanging on a wall instead of hidden inside my closet I would have seen it sooner. I just knew that something about it bothered me. And now I know why. Now I see it."

"See what?"

"The way you've painted you and your sister. The expression on your face . . . you look angry, sad, scared, and worried. And your sister? She looks happy."

"She *is* happy. I'm the worrier in the family."

"Not always. You used to be happy, like she is. That changed," Nicki said.

"Things change. I grew up."

"It's more than that. It's what's behind the two of you. The background in your painting." She paused. "Those dark strokes, they look like fingers, like hands, reaching out, touching you, *violating* you."

I felt myself shudder, but I didn't blink, or flinch, or change my expression in the smallest way. I just kept on staring straight at the painting. I didn't want her to know what I was thinking, what I was feeling, the way my guts were rolling and raging, and how much I was fighting the urge to cry or scream or puke or run out the door.

"That's how I knew you had been cutting yourself on your thighs," she said. "Lots of kids mutilate themselves, but when they cut themselves on the legs it's usually because they've been abused . . . sexually abused."

I stared harder at the painting, not daring to look at Nicki.

"I'm not going to ask if you've been sexually abused," Nicki said, "because I *know* you have been. What I want to know is if you're safe now."

"I'm safe," I whispered.

"That's good," Nicki said. "I'm so glad you're safe. But there's one other thing I need to know about. Look at the picture."

There was no need to say that to me because I couldn't take my eyes off it.

"The darkness that's in the picture, the part that's engulfing you, surrounding you." She paused. "Do you see the way it's starting to extend toward your sister . . . how the fingers are moving toward her? Do you see that?"

I gasped. I'd painted it but I'd never seen it, I'd never really looked at it myself. There they were, the dark strokes moving toward her. My God.

"Dana, this is important," Nicki said. "Has your sister been abused?"

"No . . . I . . . I . . . I don't think so . . . no, I don't think so . . . not when I left," I stammered.

"Are you sure?"

"I'm sure. She would have told me. She tells me everything. She couldn't keep that a secret."

"Didn't you keep it a secret?"

My guts started to roll around even more violently.

"Is she in danger?" Nicki asked. "Is the person who abused you still in the house?"

I nodded. "My stepfather. But he never touched her. I *know* he didn't."

"There's lots of things you can't know for certain," she said.

She was right. How could I know about my sister if my mother didn't know about me?

"When did the abuse start with you, Dana?" Nicki asked.

"A long time ago," I said. "Almost four years ago."

"How old were you?"

"Eleven."

"And how old is your sister now?"

"She's ten . . . no, eleven . . . she just had her birthday." I felt like my heart was stuck in my throat, like I couldn't breathe.

Nicki reached over and took my hand. "Dana," she said. I looked away from the painting and at her. I was panic-stricken. "We have to do something. Something to protect your sister."

"I can't do anything. I couldn't even protect myself."

"We have to protect her."

"I can't. I can't go back," I stammered.

"Nobody's asking you to go back, but we have to do something. Dana, do you trust me?" Nicki asked.

"I guess."

"Then you have to trust me to do the right thing—the right thing for you and your sister. This isn't going to be easy."

"Nothing ever is," I said. "Ever."

"And I'll be there to help, every step of the way," she said.

I took a deep, deep breath. "Do what you need to do . . . what we need to do for my sister."

chapter twenty-one

"DO I LOOK OKAY?" I asked Becca nervously.

"You look fine, very nice."

"But do I look like an artist?"

Becca laughed. "Do you mean do you have enough piercings and tattoos?"

I groaned. "I don't have any tattoos, and the only parts I have that are pierced are my ears."

She laughed. "Don't worry about it. I have enough piercings for both of us, and I just got a new tattoo." She rolled up her sleeve to show off the new artwork, a beautiful design that went all around her upper arm. I was guessing she'd drawn it herself.

"It's nice, but I don't think I'll ever get a tattoo."

"Probably smart. My mother says she remembers when getting a tattoo was a sign of rebellion, not conformity."

"What exactly does that mean?" I asked.

"It means don't get a tattoo unless *you* really want one. It's not about keeping up with your friends or looking like an artist or being anybody but yourself," she explained. "And tonight is all about the art, and your painting is going to wow them. So, you ready?"

"I guess."

"Then take a deep breath and let's go."

Becca pulled back the curtain that separated the backroom from the gallery and we stepped through. All around us on all the walls were paintings. Most of them were Becca's, and I was familiar with a lot of them. That didn't mean I wasn't impressed, or disturbed—Becca said it was hard to do one without the other. There were also paintings by other artists, and of course *my* painting. It was hanging on its own. Becca said it was in a very, very good location in the gallery.

Interspersed among the paintings were pieces of abstract sculpture. They were made of old computers and TV sets, scraps of metal, fast-food wrappers and containers, and broken Barbie dolls—all things that had been found in the garbage. They were welded and glued together in strange and bizarre patterns and combinations. The program for the night called them *"avant-garde, street-inspired art that makes a poignant statement about the disposability of humans and their possessions."* I just thought they were kind of strange, and not really art. But what did I know? I didn't even have any piercings and my hair wasn't pink.

There was a buzz of conversation in the room as more and more people filtered in. They were young, old, men, women, couples, singles, groups, well dressed, strangely clothed. They were everything and everybody. I couldn't help wondering what would happen if somebody took a big old glue gun and stuck all the people together into a piece of avant-garde art. I didn't know if it would look any good, but it would probably have impressed some people.

Moving among the crowd were waitresses carrying trays holding little pieces of cheese and tiny sandwiches and mini-sausages and pint-sized glasses of white wine. Everything was tiny. It was like they were trying to feed a whole bunch of leprechauns.

"Looks like a good turnout," Becca said.

"There *are* a lot of people," I said.

"The more people who come, the more they are willing to spend, and the more paintings get sold."

"Do you think mine's going to sell?"

"I'd bet money on it. But I do have one suggestion. Don't stand by your painting."

"Why not?"

"Because other people are going to be standing there talking about it, and while some of them will like it tremendously, some will really, *really* not like it at all."

"Why wouldn't they like it?"

"Because that's the way it is. If they were showing the *Mona Lisa* here tonight there'd be at least three people who would think it's a piece of garbage. You'll save yourself a lot of irritation if you don't stand there to hear those three stupid people talk."

"If you want, I'll stay in the kitchen for the whole evening," I offered.

"Becca, darling!" a woman screamed from the far side of the gallery. She waved her hand in the air, barged through people, and came toward us. She was wearing tight pants, a low-cut top, hair piling up to the sky, and lots and lots of jewellery.

"My agent," Becca said.

"You have an agent?"

"Yeah, and if you're not careful you'll end up with her as your agent, too."

"How are you, darling?" She threw her arms around Becca and gave her a kiss on both cheeks.

"I'm good," Becca said.

"Excellent! This is a wonderful night, wonderful!"

"I hope so."

"We have so much to discuss."

"I'll leave you two to talk," I suggested.

"Thank you, young lady. And would you be a dear and bring me a drink?"

"She's not a waitress," Becca said.

"Oh, I'm sorry . . . my apologies."

"I'll catch up to you," Becca said. "And remember to stay away from your painting, Dana."

"Dana? Are you Dana?" the agent asked.

I nodded.

"We simply *have* to talk. Becca has told me all about you! Right after Becca and I finish up our discussion I'll come and track you down!"

"Okay . . . sure." Somehow being tracked down by her didn't sound like something I really wanted. Maybe it wasn't too late to get her a drink and pretend I really was a waitress.

I wandered off into the crowd. I didn't know if anybody was actually going to buy anything, but they certainly did seem to be enjoying themselves. They were eating miniature food, drinking tiny drinks, talking, and laughing. I wished I had somebody to laugh with and talk to and—just then the door opened and Ashley and Brent and Gizmo and Nicki walked in!

I rushed over. "It's so great to see you all!" I exclaimed. "I'm so glad you could come!"

"Wouldn't miss it for the world," Brent said, giving me a hug. "You know art is my life."

"Yeah, right. So tell me about your life," I said. "How are things going?"

"We're doing amazing. You have to come and see our new apartment," Ashley said.

"You got it?" I exclaimed.

"Two bedrooms above a store on Queen Street."

"That's amazing, that's wonderful! And how about Pumpkin? How is she doing?" Ashley had promised that as soon as they had an apartment Pumpkin wouldn't be homeless either. "I can't wait to see her again."

"You probably won't recognize her," Brent said.

"Why not?"

"Because Ashley's been feeding her so much that the cat's gotten fat," he said.

"She has put on a little weight," Ashley admitted.

"A little?" Brent questioned. "She's been spoiling that animal!"

"Pumpkin deserves to be spoiled. I'm making up for the years she wasn't treated right."

"If you're not careful, you're going to kill her with kindness," Brent said. "Poor cat's so overweight she's a candidate for a cat cardiac arrest."

"She's just pleasantly plump, and I'm going to keep on spoiling her. Why shouldn't I? She's my baby . . . mine and Dana's."

"And how is business?" I asked Brent.

"Couldn't be better. Me and the Giz here sold three scooters last week. That's two months' rent with enough left over to buy pieces for three more scooters."

"I'm so proud of you both."

"So when are you coming over to see our place?" Brent asked.

"She'll have to check to make sure she's allowed," Nicki said.

"She's right, I have to ask permission before I go anywhere," I said.

"From your foster parents?" Brent asked.

"Them and the social worker . . . *my* social worker. They watch over me pretty carefully."

"That's good, I guess. How are things going?" Ashley asked.

"Okay. They've been foster parents for a long time so they know what they're doing," I said.

"And they're treating you okay?" Brent said.

"Yeah. They're nice people."

"'Cause if they're not treating you right, you know you've got a place to stay."

"If things aren't going well she can talk to her social worker," Nicki pointed out. "She's not going to be running anywhere, right?"

"Right," I said. "Anyway, I don't think I'm going to be in foster care for too much longer . . . I might be going home . . . to be with my sister."

"And your mother too, right?" Ashley asked.

I nodded. "She's there."

"And your stepfather is gone now?" Brent asked.

"Gone forever." He'd been arrested, I explained, and the deal was that when he was eventually let out he'd have to live someplace else. He wasn't even allowed near the house. That was probably a good thing, because my mother said she'd kill him if she ever saw him again.

"But if he's gone, why don't you just go home now?" Brent asked.

I'd asked myself that same question hundreds of times, and each time I'd got the same answer. "I'm not ready. Not yet, but maybe soon. I've been home for visits, and I talk to my mother and sister on the phone all the time. But not yet."

I didn't want to talk any more about any of that. "I'm just so glad that things are working out so well for all of you."

"Couldn't be better," Brent said. "We have a place to live, and our business is up and running."

"Thanks to Nicki's help," Ashley said.

"I didn't do much," Nicki said.

"She helped to get us a government grant to buy the materials to set up our business," Gizmo explained.

"All part of the job," she said.

Brent looked around. "What does a hard-working man have to do to get something to eat around here? There is food, right? I was promised there would be food."

"There's food," I reassured him. Miniature food, but it was food.

"Enough talk, it's time to chow down!" Brent and Gizmo spotted one of the waitresses circulating on the far side of the room and made a beeline in her direction.

"Maybe I'd better just keep an eye on the two of them so they don't eat everything in sight," Ashley said, smiling, and she headed off to join the boys.

"I'm so glad they came," I told Nicki. "I love them so much. I'm so glad everything is working out for them. It wouldn't be right for me to be safe if they were still out there on the streets."

"They're going to make it," Nicki said, "Are things *really* going well for you?"

"As good as they can. Sometimes it's tough."

"But you are getting through it?"

"Trying to."

"And your mother . . . is she trying too?"

I nodded. "Really hard."

"It's all right that you're still angry at her."

"I was never angry at . . ." I stopped myself mid-sentence. "I'm not as angry as I was."

"Anger is natural. But try to remember, she was a victim too. Have you been seeing your mother and sister often?"

"A few times a week. I even slept at home last Saturday."

"And how did that go?"

"It wasn't easy. I hardly slept at all. It just didn't feel safe being in my room again."

Nicki nodded knowingly. "Did you talk to your social worker about it?"

"A little bit."

"It sounds like those are the sorts of things that you should expect. Be patient with yourself, and don't be too proud to ask for help," she said.

"I don't know what I would have done without *your* help."

She smiled. "I didn't do that much."

"Yes you did. Without you, none of this would have happened for any of us."

Nicki shook her head. "I just helped a bit, helped with the outline . . . the rough draft . . . the sketch. Filling the painting with colour and making it come to life, that's up to you."

"I just hope I can do it," I said.

"You can. Just remember, there are people who care." She paused. "People like that," she said, glancing over my shoulder.

I turned around. It was my mother. She had told me she would come, but it still surprised me to see her there. This was part of a world that I'd come to know, not the world where she and I knew each other.

"She really does care for you," Nicki said. "You have to learn that forgiving is different from forgetting. And I don't mean just forgiving your mother, but yourself."

Nicki reached over and put a hand on my shoulder, and it almost felt like some of her strength, some of her wisdom, rushed into me.

"I'm going to look at the artwork now," Nicki said. "I'll talk to you later."

Nicki walked away, leaving me alone in the crowd. I looked over to where my mother stood. She was alone in the crowd too. She still hadn't seen me. She looked anxious, unsure of herself, scared, alone. I knew all those feelings from the inside.

She looked over and saw me and our eyes met. She smiled and I smiled back. Suddenly she didn't look so scared or alone. And suddenly I didn't feel so scared or alone either.